James Buchanan Elmore

Love among the Mistletoe and Poems

James Buchanan Elmore

Love among the Mistletoe and Poems

ISBN/EAN: 9783744707947

Printed in Europe, USA, Canada, Australia, Japan

Cover: Foto ©Andreas Hilbeck / pixelio.de

More available books at **www.hansebooks.com**

James B. Elmore

At 20 years of age.

Love Among the Mistletoe

AND

Poems

BY

JAMES B. ELMORE

ALAMO, IND.:
PUBLISHED BY THE AUTHOR.
1899

PREFACE.

This book is dedicated to all lovers of good,
  And to those who admire pure reading.
Be sure to peruse it as you should,
  Observing the lessons of good breeding.
We give no apology for making things plain,
  In a modest, graphical way.
For nature has done her work just the same,
  And given our lessons to-day.
Mother Nature has been to us a great school,
  Of which ourselves are a part.
There can be no offense, if we stick to the rule,
  And give the pen-pictures of heart.
Now this we have done for the pleasure of all,
  And to the inanimate gave life.
We deem it the best new things to install
  And give to Dame Nature new life.

JAMES B. ELMORE.

INDEX.

LOVE AMONG THE MISTLETOE.

Railroad Station, Fairmount

A LONG a winding river, where grew forests of chestnut, magnolia and elm, many years ago, a very rich man settled and bought a large tract of land, lying on each side of this beautiful stream. He lived here in solitude for a number of years on his vast estate, lying on either side of the great Rock River, stretching for miles up and down the stream, clothed in the most picturesque scenery.

But one fine day a son was born to him, and was christened John Arno. He was a very beautiful child, and heir to all the estate. The plantation grew and grew, and became more attractive as a public resort, as the adjoining lands were cleared and made into farms. Around this place a great many incidents cling. The old man and woman were of Quaker descent, and were very odd. They had a kind of an aversion to society, but they built for them-

2

(1)

selves a palace on the highest bank of the river, or in
other words it was a vast citadel. One had but to
look out and behold the river below, with its nar-
rows and whispering galleries as the winds gently
passed by.

In this pleasant situation John grew to manhood,
playing along the river, hunting pretty shells, and
climbing the hills, which teemed with wild flowers,
corded grape-vines and mistletoe. He would take his
hook and line, and would fish for bass, silversides and
gold fish. He would sit on a very large rock in the
river, known as the Old Eagle Rock, where the last
wild Indian was shot and killed by a neighbor while
he was fishing. The Indian incurred the enmity of
this man by telling stories of vast lead mines on the
plantation, whose location he kept a secret, and by
telling how he had killed white people and infant
children by taking them by the feet and knocking
their brains out against the walls of their houses, and
as you know by tradition even back to the ancients.
The blood of this Indian is on this rock to-day as it
gushed forth and he plunged into the river. John
would take long rambles in the woods, and he became
acquainted with the different kinds of wild flowers
which grew on every knoll and hill. The creeks and
rills rippled over mossy beds and pebbly bottoms
which sparkled like diamonds.

On the north bank of Rock River was a large cave,

known as Hidden Mystery, where oft John and the people would go with lanterns and torches as explorers. This cave had many rooms and domes, with sweet waters. The water which trickled down the walls left them encrusted, which shone all around like stars or rubies when exposed to the light of the lanterns. The water which trickled down overhead left spires as clear as crystal, and in the bottom were porous rock and eyeless fish.

Now, John was old enough to go to school, but he had been born and raised in one of Nature's grandest of art schools in the world. His father determined to send him to school at Boston, where he could add to his natural learning a scientific knowledge and come in contact with the wealth and pomp of the old world among the gay ladies and jeweled princesses. The day came, and John, with his father, embarked on a steamer for Boston. Down the great Mississippi they go to the Gulf of Mexico, where they embark on a large vessel for New York, and thence to Boston. In about a week they are in Boston, and John is sent to college, where he is to stay five years, or until he is twenty years old. His father goes home and engages in stocks and bonds and pork-packing, and it seemed as though he had the touch of the fabled Midas, as everything he touched turned into the yellow metal.

But, as you have learned, this is one of the prettiest places in the world, with its semi-tropical scenery,

and it being a favorite watering-place, people from
all over the world came on tours of pleasure and en-
vied the old man his possessions, and young lasses
sought the hand of his son. There was a great
bridge across Rock River at this place, where people

THE CASTLE.

would cross and linger for hours and hours looking at
the scenery, and the great mansion which overlooked
the crowning hill. In these days it was something
uncommon to see such a large building in this section
of country, and such elevators of stored grain. In
the cellar of this grand mansion was everything that

man could wish—all kinds of fruits and viands. There were malt liquors which had grown old with age, and which had become thick and white like cream, and lost their tart, biting sting, such as epicures would like to sample. The barrels were covered with moss like that on the rock of ages.

Now, this toiling father was growing old, and his very dream was the idol of his son, on whom he wished to bestow all his wealth—not only the treasures of this earth, but the treasures of his heart also. And the mother—a meek, gentle woman, polished and mannerly, a very type of beauty and of her race. It seems as though wealth is an incentive to bring the beautiful of earth together, which begets beauty until it is in a perfect state, enabling one to grow in ease and pleasure, and therefore grow to manhood and obtain those luxuries and necessities which are builders of symmetry. The mother has impressed upon her son the kind, gentle spirit of her life, and is looking forward to the crowning of her glory.

John has now gone to college for two years, and has made many acquaintances, and has looked upon many fair faces. He has been leader in his class, having inherited the will-power of his father, and he has refused the hand of many fair ladies. But in the midst of his success his father dies, leaving all in his hands; but his mother is to assume control of the estate until he is twenty-one years of age. He is

called home to the funeral of his father, and stays a
week for recreation, and during this week at home he
returns to his old playgrounds amidst the hills and
vines along the creek, and in one of his rambles he
spies a neat, beautiful form standing on the bank of
the stream and looking at him. He looks again, and
he is bewildered with the brightness of her face. He
had never looked upon such a one before. A feeling
of love came over him as she tossed at him a red rose
that he could not resist. His large blue eyes peered
into hers, which were a beautiful brown, and there
was such a charm in them that he waded across the
stream to greet her, and, climbing up the little
hillock, he bowed and introduced himself as Mr. John
Arno, of Kingston. She also bowed with courtesy
and said: "Miss Violet Payne, of Queenstown," and
her voice closed with a musical Scottish accent which
he never forgot—that voice he could hear at all times.
It was to him like that of the sweet sirens of the
lonely isles.

The happy meeting was like that which befalls
some awful catastrophe. For a moment all was silent
while each looked upon the other. Then he said:
"Let's take a ramble and cull some pretty flowers."
They started off on a tour of the hills and valleys,
seeking the pretty flowers and shells, and walked
along Echoing Glen, whose upright walls rebounded
the human voice, and where the wild pheasants beat

upon their breasts with their wings, which seemed
like the distant sound of some primeval drum. Then
as they retraced their steps the quail whistled a signal
of approaching eve, and the whip-poor-will darted
here and there. On arriving at her carriage they
agreed to correspond with each other when he arrived
at school and she at her home. Then the driver was
ready, and a crack of the whip sent the carriage rolling away over the pike, while he stood in low spirits,
watching the one object of his mind vanish out of
sight.

He returned to his home at Kingston late in the
evening. His mother discovered that he did not act
with as much high spirits as usual, but she supposed
that it was owing to the death of his father and his
having to return to school on the morrow. He as-
sisted his mother with her work as best he could, and
appeared to be as cheerful as one could under the
circumstances. His mother noticed, too, that there
was an expression of absent-mindedness in his demeanor, and she meditated herself as to the cause of
it. She thought that if her son appeared so at school
that he would do no good, but she hoped and trusted
for the better.

John went to bed with a light heart, and he could
hear that vessel beat and throb at his breast with
greater ardor than usual. He lay on his bed with
his mind's eye placed upon the object which he had

seen across the flowing river and standing like a
statue on the little hillock. But as his anxiety was
worn away he passed into deep repose, thinking little
of the future. That bed was to him like the bed of
shamrock and roses to the daughter of Daniel
O'Connell on the banks of the Sharon in the Emerald
Isle. But on his awaking he felt like he was transported from a land of sweet dreams, and went about
greeting his mother and getting his many things together for his return to school. His mother tried to
be in his presence as much as possible, for she knew
how long two years of absence would be, and as she
was getting old she might not survive that time But
all seemed well for the time. She knew she would
have to spend her time with the servants and make
the most of life, for her husband, Mr. Arno, was a
cheerful man, jolly and sociable.

The time for his departure had come, and George,
the old servant of the family, who had been so good
and trusty for so many years, had the best team of
roadsters hitched to take him to the station. He
walked out to the carriage, while his baggage was
carried by the servant. His mother followed to bid
him good-bye, and to give him a check for $500, his
yearly allowance set apart by his father. As he took
the check he shook hands with his mother, and tears
stood in his bright blue eyes so large that they
dimmed his sight, and his mother could scarcely bear

up under the sadness of heart. George had already seated himself in the carriage, and John, springing in, seated himself by his side. As George pulled the reins they are off immediately.

It is twenty miles to the station, but John gets George to go by way of Queenstown, which is about five miles out of the way, so that he may see the home of Violet, and, if possible, get a glimpse of her. George wonders why John wanted to go that way, but hesitated to interrogate him. About a mile north of Queenstown is a quaint little cottage, surrounded by chestnuts and evergreens, and whose lawns were decorated with smilax, honeysuckles and chrysanthemums. It recalls to one the scene of Maud Muller's beautiful country home, as portrayed by the artful mind of Whittier. As they approach this lovely place they behold a beautiful little cottage, like that of a shepherd in Scotland. George notices that John is restless, and is constantly looking in the distant yard. Violet is near where the lambkins are at play, amusing herself with these gentle animals. They are driving very fast, and John salutes her with his handkerchief; but she does not fully recognize him, but thinks it resembles the heir at Kingston. George for the first time has his suspicion aroused, for he too saw the beautiful physique of the lady, which to him was an ideal of symmetry. They speed along, and John gives George a faint idea of his friendship's

episode, trusting him to keep the secret. Now, this
was like a bomb to George, as he had never seen John
in the company of ladies. They arrive at the station:
it is after noon and the train is on time, and their
words of parting are few. He hands to George a
sweet-scented Havana cigar, and requests him to give
his mother his best love and esteem, and asks him to
keep his secret. The train has now arrived: they
shake hands, and John is off for the Mississippi and
George to the grief-stricken home, where he finds
Mrs. Arno awaiting his arrival, and the incidents of
her son's departure. When everything is attended
to they seat themselves and George relates how cheerfully they made the trip, and how John got on the
train and it glided off with the wings of a bird. But
he never once hinted of the beautiful peasant home
which they had passed. Mrs. Arno was a kind, gentle
woman, and had no dislike for the poor or those who
were less fortunate than herself. But she well knew
the position wealth placed one in in society, and so
she desired her son to marry a lady of wealth. She
went about her work in the same industrious manner
that she had always done, and George had to assume
the responsibility and care of the estate under her
supervision.

In a few days John arrived at school, and went
about his work with ardor, for he was ambitious and
filled with zeal. He met all his old friends and

treated them as best he could in the condition he was placed by the death of his father and the parting of his new acquaintance. He assumed rather the habits of a Thoreau, but he was always at the head of his class. The time passed away very fast, and one evening, while meditating, he resolved to write to Violet, and, seating himself at his table, which was strewn with the sophomore's books, he attempted to write her a letter, but their acquaintance was so brief that he hardly knew what to write. So he wrote a neat letter of friendship, rehearsing their first meeting and their ramble over hills and valleys, which he so much enjoyed, and would some time in the future be pleased to see her again, and of the favorable impression he had formed of her. He also related to her his long trip, and how he went from place to place until he arrived at Boston. He requested her to write soon, and closed with these beautiful lines:

How sweet it is to me, I find,
To live in hearts we leave behind.

Your friend,
JOHN ARNO,
Boston, Mass.

In due time Violet received this letter and read it with care, noting everything, even the style and expression. She kept it all a secret, for she had a fellow by the name of Cecil Ivy, who had been courting

her for a long time, and who was well-to-do and very
good looking, and who had many friends, and of
whom Violet thought very well. She made up her
mind to write Mr. Arno a letter, thanking him very
much for the high esteem in which he held her, and
acknowledging the receipt of his very welcome letter.
She told him of her trip home from Rock River, and
how she admired the grandeur of the scenery, and she
closed by soliciting an answer and signing:

Your friend,
Miss Violet Payne,
Queenstown, Tenn.

She has a lady friend by the name of Fay Larchen
in whom she places confidences, and often trusted her
with her secrets. In a few days she meets Fay, and
they go for a ramble in the orchard near the old well,
where the ancient shadoosh overhangs the curb, with
a moss-covered vessel attached to the end of a pole,
the like of which would suggest a good place to tell
one's secrets. Here Violet narrates to Fay her trip
to the river, her meeting of John Arno and their
pleasant walk, and her promise to write to him when
he arrived in Boston. She shows John's letter, and
Fay is so fascinated with it that she wants to write to
John, as Violet already has a gentleman friend.
Violet does not consent, although she thinks well of
Cecil, and trusts all will be well. Fay, being defeated in her wish, confides her secret to Cecil, which

is bound to create a jealousy. Cecil now goes to see Violet, who seems to be as cheerful as ever and treats him with as much courtesy. But he pushes his suit more than ever, and accuses her of another gentleman friend. She acknowledges the receipt of a letter, but that 'twas only a friendship one. Cecil makes greater appeals of love, and asks her hand, but she withholds her answer. He still comes to see her, and her mother tells her that she is getting old, and that she will need an arm upon which to lean, when she is gone; also, Fay tries to induce her to accept, but she can't decide.

Violet now sees a rival in Fay, if she but gives her the opportunity. So she is a little shy until she is more settled in her mind. But during this time she receives another letter from John acknowledging the receipt of hers. He is now some encouraged, and has recovered from home affairs, and his pen glows with a gentle ripple of harmony. He tells her how he is getting along, and hopes he may be home soon. He closed again with a few lines on their first meeting:

> The day that I stood beside the brook,
>   And thou stood on the hill,
> I gave but one mild, gentle look,
>   Whilst thou stood still.

>   Answer soon.
>   Your friend,
>   JOHN ARNO,
>   Boston, Mass.

Violet does not show this letter, and Cecil comes
on and presses his suit, and Violet does not know ex-
actly what to do. She knows that Cecil loves her,
but she is not certain about John, as he has been very
delicate, and she does not know that she is the only
lady friend he ever had.

Cecil asks her to take a drive out to Rock River,
and she consents. The day is set, and they drive out.
They go up and down the river, and view Paradise
Alley, where the scenes are as beautiful as the word
implies, with its little stream flowing over shining
pebbles, and a narrow path extending along each side,
with such pretty mosses and hanging vines that one
nearly loses consciousness. While here, Cecil thinks
he may overcome her obstinacy, and he talks of the
future, and his love for her, and hopes she may consent to his proposal; but she drops the conversation
by alluding to their pleasant surroundings. They
pass on and come to Pleasant View, where they as-
cend a little mound opposite a beautiful cascade,
whose waters fall about twenty feet and turn in a boil
below, forming a white foam, and a gentle zephyr
carries a mist into the air, on which is mirrored all
the prismatic colors of the rainbow.

In this picturesque place Cecil says in his heart:
"This world would I give, were it mine, for the hand
of Violet." George, the old servant, is looking over
the estate, and sees these two young people, and

watches them. He thinks he recognizes the form he saw at the peasant cottage, and he knows by their actions that they are lovers. They pass on and arrive at a cliff, where the old eagles are feeding their young, and the whole cliff seems to be perforated or honey-combed. Then they arrive at the little hillock where she first met John Arno, and she pauses and looks down upon the spot where he stood, gazing in space, speechless, thinking: "Was it true, or is it only a fancy, such as lovers are apt to have?" Cecil notices this, and he is spellbound to know what it means. Violet sees in her mind's eye that tall, graceful form standing there, and says to herself, "I would he could be there now." George, by this strange incident, is certain that it is Violet, and that there is a strain upon her mind—something that is clothed in mystery or hidden in the deep recesses of the soul. Cecil and Violet pass on, but Violet is not cheerful, and they go to the carriage and return home. Cecil does the talking, while she is meditating, only now and then assenting to what he says. They part at the gate with the same friendship as before. Cecil has accused her of her love for some other one, but she keeps her secrets. He goes home and gets Fay Larchen to visit Violet, and they repair to the old swing in the orchard to talk over old times, and Fay tries to solicit Violet to tell her more about John; but Violet is wise in her own counsel, and she is reticent.

Then Fay shows the good qualities of Cecil, and Violet admits its being so. Fay also talks to Violet's mother, and tries in that way to find out something. But as yet she knows little of Violet's meeting John. George, the servant, writes to John what he saw, and tells all he knows about the circumstances, and describes the man which he saw with her the best that he can, and about her standing on the little hillock, gazing on the shoal of pebbles, mussel and periwinkle shells.

It has been some time since Violet received a letter, and she now, since she has taken the pleasure trip and has been relieved from the pressure of friends, seats herself to write to John. She relates her trip to Rock River and the pleasant time she had, and recalls the place of their first meeting so long ago. She tells how many young people she saw boating and moving slowly down the stream with the current, and the gay laughter that echoed in her ears. But she never once says a word of her gentleman friend who accompanied her. She makes herself appear as happy as possible, and hopes he is so in the Hub City in a whirlpool of society, and closes with a very friendly greeting.

Little does she know of the strain on his mind to get an education and become famous, and of his seclusion from society. He has received George's letter some days before, and he knows, when he receives

Violet's letter, that George is true and faithful, and that he really saw Violet at the dells. John is worried about the gentleman that George saw with her, but he makes up his mind never to say a word to her about it, and trusts to silence as the best road to long friendship, as it will be more manly and let his affections pass to her heart as the seraphs take their flight from earth to heaven. And he well knows, in the language of Shakespeare, that "light winning makes the prize light." So he studies on, with a little fear in his heart lest he fail in his love. He writes to his dear mother and George, telling his situation, and how he is advancing in his studies, and speaks of his being well, and thanks George for his many favors so that his mother will not understand what he has reference to. He now writes to Violet, acknowledging the receipt of her ever-welcome letter, and the happiness which it gave him to hear from her and that life was a pleasure to her. But he thought that he needed some assistance to counteract Fay in her work for Cecil. So he writes to his cousin, Agnes Percy, at Oaken, a nice letter, and sends his picture, requesting her to go and make the acquaintance of Violet and to give her the picture, and tell her of his deep love which he has for her, and to see if Violet returned his affection.

Now, Agnes was a good messenger, for she was well received by Violet, and her very face bore the impres-

3

sion of confidence, and, as you know, when one is in
love and troubled, they are low-spirited and apt to tell
secrets. They went to the orchard, so as to be alone,
and to talk together. Agnes drew from her bosom
the photograph of John and handed it to Violet, who,
on recognizing it, pressed it to her lips and kissed it.
Then she leaned over and embraced Agnes. This act
sealed their friendship. Agnes knew well that Violet
loved, and as she was John's cousin, she no longer
hid it from her. She told Agnes that she loved Cecil,
but had not consented to his proposal, and that she
thought well of John also, but that she did not know
whether he would return her love. So Agnes told
her how much John was infatuated with her, and to
wait awhile before she made up her mind, and that
John was delicate on such matters, and how he had
solicited her to assist him, and that she thought him
in earnest. So Violet said she would defer answering
Cecil for some time. Then Agnes returned home and
wrote to John what she had done and what she had
found out. Then John thought, that he was all right
if he could come home soon. His school will soon
close, and he will be one of the best in his class, and
he can begin life for himself with honor.

Cecil kept on going with Violet as before, and kept
the same old struggle in her heart alive. She did not
feel like casting him off, for fear of the worst, and so
it filled her very soul with gloom, and her mother sug-

gested that Cecil was all right and would make a good husband, but Violet said nothing, which only made her the more miserable. Her heart burst to tell her secret, but she dare not. If she could but see Agnes and relieve herself of her load, she would give all she possessed. She would get in the carriage and go, but she would have to pass Cecil's home, and that would give her away: so she must smother the burning flame within her breast.

School is now about to close, and John's mother is sick, and he is anxious to return. John's mother recalled to George the sadness of her son when he left home, and wondered why it was. George remarked that it might be a love affair, but said no more. As the school neared a close, days were as months. His mother was growing weaker, and John must go home to see her. George notifies him of his mother's condition, and informs him that she is only convalescent, and to fear not, for he will care for her.

John remains at school until its close, and graduates. He then packs his things for home—the dearest spot to him on earth! No one knows what home is until away in a distant land, and let remorse come over them, or get disheartened—and John has experienced all of this. His goods are expressed to the wharf, and John embarks on a great Atlantic steamer for New Orleans, where he takes a Mississippi steamboat for home. He arrives at Fairmount station, and

George is there, according to a prearrangement which they had consummated. John asks George to go by way of Oaken, so that he may see Agnes and learn all about Violet that he can. They arrive at Oaken and they go in, and his cousin and aunt are glad to see them. John asks Agnes about Violet, and Agnes tells him she is the finest lady she ever met, so nice and accomplished, but that he may have hard work to win her, and that Cecil is still keeping her company. Agnes tells him she is a perfect type of womanhood. John then requests Agnes to visit Violet frequently, and to give her his best respects, and inform her of how much admiration he has for her, and that he will be very reticent, and that he thinks he can succeed better in that way, as it will deceive Cecil and Fay if he is not seen about Queenstown. It will be hard for him to stay away. but he has great will-power and can control himself in that matter. He also requests her to visit him soon at Kingston, and that his mother will be glad to see her.

He then starts for home, where he finds his mother improving in health, and she is very glad to see him, and to give the management of the estate over to him and relieve her mind from its care. The mother is glad to know that her son is a graduate, and thinks she sees a bright future before him, for, as Solomon has said, "A wise son maketh a glad father," it follows that the mother would be glad also,

John looks over the estate to see what is needed, but his mind is not content, and he often finds himself wandering as if in dreamland. He has never been in such a condition before, and he thinks it is on account of his affection for Violet, and he is contemplating as to how he will propose to her, and he wants to do it in the best manner that he possibly can. He sends for Agnes to come and visit him at the castle, and then he thinks he may see some way out of the difficulty. George is dispatched for Agnes, and told to call on Violet as he returns, and have Agnes to converse with her and tell her of his unrest of mind, and that he must see her soon. When George reaches Agnes's house she is as happy as a lark and pleased to make the visit. Her mother assists her to get ready and gives her permission to stay for a fortnight. When they are ready they are off for the visit. They soon arrive at Violet's home, and find the same grand personage busy with the things about her home. Violet welcomes them in, and George makes the acquaintance of Mrs. Payne and converses with her while Agnes talks with Violet, and speaks to her about John and his condition of mind, and says that she may send for her while she is at the Arno castle, and she consents to come. Violet sends her best respects to John, and her picture. Mrs. Payne thinks strange of this proceeding, and begins to question Violet about their calling; but she has a level head, and avoids the matter by telling her mother that it was only a friendly visit. But Mrs. Payne is not perfectly satisfied in her own mind.

George and Agnes go on to the Arno home, and find John and Mrs. Arno very glad to see them. What a bright, cheerful girl Agnes is! It makes one happy to be in her presence, and Mrs. Arno is much better by Agnes's coming to see her. As soon as Agnes and Mrs. Arno converse awhile, John seeks an opportunity to speak to her about Violet. They go to the parlor, and while looking at the pictures on the center table John asks about Violet. Agnes tells John that Violet sent her best respects to him, and, opening her valise, took out a picture and gave it to him, and a mingled feeling of surprise and wonder came over him. His mind is carried back by the beautiful photograph to the little hillock where first he saw her standing like a beautiful flower which the dew of morn had caressed, and, standing among these beautiful environments, the brilliant rays of the sun only added splendor to the scene that he beheld; and, recovering himself, he said:

"Agnes, this is the most beautiful picture that I ever saw. It is so like Violet—so modest, so charming. She is the only lady that I ever met whose personal appearance has had such a control over me. She has changed my whole life. You know how I used to ramble in the woods and dells by myself, and perfectly happy; but now I am not. I must see Violet soon, or I fear that Cecil will overcome her and make my life miserable. I have trusted to you, Agnes, my most profound secrets, and relied on you to secure the information which would win me the prize and make me happy. I hope you have done all you could, for there is no other person I would like to trust so well."

Agnes thanks him for the confidence which he places in her. She assures him that what she tells him is true, and that he can win her if he only proceeds in earnest before she would consent to wed Cecil, and that she has been delaying to answer Cecil to hear from him. So he arranges to go and see her and find out some of her parentage, and become better convinced of her beauty and surroundings. So he gets ready and goes on Thursday. He thinks it is a lucky day, and that he may avoid meeting Cecil, as he would be likely to be there on Sunday, for he has not ceased to woo her.

When John arrives he sees her at a distance watering the beautiful lawn which surrounds the neat little country home. She knows him, and quits her work and comes to meet him. They greet each other very cheerfully, and talk of the pleasant day, and of the most cheerful things one could think of. She tells him she is so glad that he came, as she had wanted to see him for so long and talk of their first happy meet-

ing. which seemed to her like a miracle.   He cannot
help but show his appreciation of her, and she knows
full well how to act. which adds to her personal
charms.   He is invited into the house and introduced
to Mrs. Payne, who receives him with kindness.   This
is the first time she has ever seen him. but now she
knows what has made Violet act so strange with
Cecil.   She can't help but admire the manly courage
and conversation of John.   His very demeanor is par
excellence. which makes him attractive to anyone.

Mrs. Payne converses with him awhile. and then
retires from the room and leaves Violet alone with
him.   They spend the time pleasantly, talking of the
many beautiful things which they saw the day of their
ramble along the river.   John relates many things
which occurred at Boston during his stay there, and
the life of one in the city. and of the gay people in
their gaudy dress.   But presently the conversation
changes to friendship affairs.   John relates to her
that he has heard that she has another suitor, and she
acknowledges that she has. and that he is nice. kind
and agreeable. but that she has greater admiration
for him than Cecil. and that she did not desire to
mistreat him, and that she only used courtesy in going with him.   John acts in his selfsame manner. and
says no harm of Cecil. as some rivals are wont to do
John is perfect in the art of reading human nature,
and knows that the least said the easier mended, and

that stillness makes a wise head. It is in this way
that he has had such an influence over the object of
his love, for she could not resist his manly composure,
for it was a tell-tale expression which lingered long
in her heart. It shows that it is true that persons, on
meeting, either like or dislike. There are certain
features that charm the windows of the soul which
cannot be resisted. He does not ask her to quit going
with Cecil, but leaves that to her pleasure. He says
that he may give her an invitation to visit him at the
castle while Agnes is there, and she says she would
be pleased to do so, and says that she admires the
scenes along the river, and especially the great bridge,
where she had stood for hours and hours watching the
fish jump up out of the water. He requests her not
to tell anyone of his visit, and that stillness is the best,
and that it will allay gossip. He speaks well of her
widowed mother, and thanks her for the kindness
which he had received at her home. Then he gets
ready to return home, and Violet goes with him to the
gate, where they bid each other good-bye in the way
which is the custom of lovers. John leaves no engagement, as he expects to see her at his home some
time soon.

He returns home better pleased than ever, as he
thinks that he is all right. He tells Agnes all about
how she received him, and that she is the means of
his success, and that she still must assist him, and that

he has made arrangements for Violet to visit them while she is with them.

"Good!" says Agnes. "When do you expect her?"

"I do not know," said John. "I intend to send you after her."

"I would be pleased to go," said Agnes.

Now, Agnes is the means by which John seeks to get Violet to come to their home. John's mother is not so well as usual, and detains her son about the house, which affords him an opportunity to plan with Agnes for Violet's coming to see them.

Cecil goes to see her on Sunday, and is treated very kindly, and he spends a pleasant evening, and talks very affectionately: but Violet tells him she has not yet made up her mind. She does not tell him of John's visit, and does not intend to now; but she fears Fay may find it out. She has confidence in Cecil, and thinks if John proposes she can make things all right with him, as he is a perfect gentleman. Her mother thinks strange of her keeping company with two such nice gentlemen, and says she had better let one go; but she uses her own pleasure in the matter.

Cecil returns home happy and calls on Fay, and asks her to visit Violet at her first opportunity and get any information that she can, thinking that some word may be dropped that he may interpret for his good. Fay goes immediately to visit Violet, and finds her as cheerful as usual. They talk at the house for awhile, and then they repair to the grove near by, where everything is lovely, and there talk things which they desire to be kept a secret. They talk of their friends and old times, which they desire to recall as they grow older and they see the world or themselves are changing. They realize that time is fleeting, and that they are transformed from girls to womanhood, and that their minds are changing from trivial things to reach out and grapple with the world. At this point of the conversation Fay speaks of their lovers, and she asks Violet if she thinks of Cecil as a future companion, and Violet says she has not yet determined, as that is a serious matter and must have some reflection. Fay, in a neat way, speaks of Cecil's character as being good and above reproach. Violet lets the conversation on this line drop, and speaks of the coming fashions, and what she would like to have for an outing dress. It is now evening, and Fay must return home, defeated in her purpose. She bids Violet good-bye, and asks her to visit her. Violet says she will, and asks her to come again.

Violet is now left alone, and she meditates as to how hard it is to withstand the pressure of friends and the cunning devices which are sometimes used which reach to one's very soul. She loves Fay, but thinks she is trying to pry into her secrets for a purpose. Violet goes about her work, and speaks to her mother about Fay making such inquiries about her affections for Cecil. She tells her mother how she answered her, and her mother told her she had done all right.

In a short time there is a carriage at the gate, and a man and a lady alighting. She cannot think who it is. She watches closely to ascertain who it is, but presently the doorbell rings and Violet opens the door. Then she recognizes Agnes and George. She shakes hands with George and kisses Agnes. She asks them to be seated. Her mother comes in and recognizes George as one who used to accompany Mr. Arno when he used to buy stock, and Agnes she knows, as she only lives a few miles away. After they pass the time of day they talk of social matters and the pleasant ride they had just taken, when Agnes relates to Violet that John had sent for her to come over with them to the Arno castle. She says that she will do so with pleasure, and speaks to her mother about it. Her mother grants her request and assists her to get ready. Everything is as pleasant as possible, and Agnes does what she can to assist Violet to get ready to go. Violet's mother thinks all may not be well, and meditates what to do. So she picks up courage and asks if she may accompany them. Their hearts beat with joy as they tell her certainly, she will be welcome. So they set about to assist her to get in readiness to go, and she makes arrangements to stay for a day or two, as she does not know how long they may be gone. When all is ready they repair to the carriage, and Violet and her mother occupy the rear seat, and Agnes and George in front. One could not help but admire Agnes, for she is as cheerful as a lark on a June morning, and her mind flits from one thing to another as they glide along over the pike. There are many beautiful landscapes as they pass along, and Violet is able to explain them all to her mother, for she has seen them many times before. It is a long ride, but the horses are fleet and they go along very lively. They speed along, up hill and down, and over the level plain. and the pleasant conversation of the young people recalls to Mrs. Payne very vividly her childhood days, when she too was fond of such excursions. They soon come in sight of the great residence of the Arnos, situated on a distant hill amidst picturesque scenery. There is a great chasm between them and the residence. where runs the clear waters of Rock River. spanned by the great bridge where Violet had been many times before, and of which she had told her mother; but she had never been at the residence on the hill, where now she was going. They soon must cross the bridge and reach their destination. The horses' feet are now popping on the bridge, and they look out and see some one looking at them. Violet is certain that she knows who it is, but she says nothing. They reach the ascent and wind slowly up the hill to the iron gate, where John is

ready to receive them.   John now sees that he is cap-
tivated, and repeats these beautiful lines:

> Here on the hill doth stand
> The stateliest mansion in all the land,
> A fairy home with lawns of green,
> Where reigns a peasant romance queen—
> Not alone of flowers and dells,
> But of the heart of one as well.

They are invited in and introduced to Mrs. Arno,
who is still convalescent. but she asks them to lay off
their things and make themselves comfortable.   Mrs.
Arno is surprised with the beauty of Violet, and at
the attention which her son pays to her.   The house
is beautifully arranged and furnished in grand style.
It is nicer than Violet has ever seen.   Mrs. Arno sets
herself about entertaining Mrs. Payne, and they become warm friends.   She leaves the young people to
take care of themselves.   They seat themselves
around the center table and look at the pictures, and
Violet comes to one taken when a boy, and looks it
over and over.   John remarks: "That is your friend."
"So I see," said Violet.   Agnes is as gay as ever, and
now and then gets in a bit of fun.   John thinks it is
near time for him to propose, but his heart ebbs quite
low. and he thinks that he can hear it beat against his
breast.   Agnes can see that there is a struggle going
on in John's breast, and would leave them alone if
she could excuse herself.   It is nearing meal time,

and she has to assist, so she gets an opportunity for retiring from the room.

John talks away more affectionately than ever, and Violet receives it with pleasure. They are by themselves until dinner time. John and Violet are invited out to dine, and Agnes, to play one of her jokes, has arranged to seat John and Violet together, while Mrs. Arno and Mrs. Payne are seated at the head of the table, and Agnes sits opposite to John and Violet. The viands are served, and all are cheerful. Agnes now and then takes a look at the young couple, as if to say, "How pretty you are! You resemble two young doves on the 14th of February." All this is flitting through her mind, and John and Violet can read it all, but it only adds beauty to the occasion. All this cunning mischief seems to be good morals, for it is a part of human nature, and Agnes has more than her share of such fun.

When dinner is over they repair to the parlor, and Agnes excuses herself to assist in clearing the table and to wash the dishes. Now, the two old people seem to have strange feelings coming over them, but neither speaks to the other about it. They think Providence has thrown these two people together, but do not dream as to how it will terminate.

While they are left alone the spark of love shines out brighter and brighter. John desires to be manly, and thinks some favorite scene of hers of which he has learned would be the best place to ask her hand, and where they can be all alone. You have possibly learned that the pulse beats at low tide just at such times when true love is bursting the anticipating heart. So John asks her to take a walk, and she accepts, and they go down to the great bridge and walk

THE BRIDGE ENGAGEMENT.

out to the middle of it, where they pause and look at the waters running beneath, a living stream, where it teems with great schools of fish, and now and then one jumps up out of the water and then drops back into the river. Here the shrubbery which lines the

banks of the stream is a living echo of birds warbling
their sweetest songs. It seems to John that they
know his feelings and are singing songs of cheer. So
in this favored spot he tells her that it is a long lane
that has no turn—meaning his course in life—and
that he is thinking of a change. He then asks her if
she would be willing to join him on life's billowy
wave. She responds, cheerfully: "With pleasure."
He then raised her left hand and placed upon the ring
finger a ring, signifying love without end. He then said:

"Violet, you see that we are standing on this bridge
which connects these two great bodies of land above
these living waters. So this tie which we have been
contracting must plight our hopes forever, bridging
over the great chasm where rolls life's raging river."

Violet then said: "If storms do come, we know
that harmony binds worlds together."

Then they return to the house in settled mind.
They seek the presence of the two mothers, where
John says:

"Mrs. Payne, I desire your daughter's hand in marriage."

She is somewhat surprised, but says: "If it pleases
you."

John turns to his mother and says:

"Mother, I have not consulted you, but I know you
have always desired me to be happy, and I know you
could not object to my betrothal to Violet."

"My son, I had desired you to marry a lady of wealth, but beauty is much more desirable with a contented mind than treasures of gold. So, my son, you have done well."

The two families are united. They talk over the wedding day and other arrangements, and agree to marry at the Arno home, for it is large and commodious. They speak of the bridesmaids, and Violet selects Agnes as one, and John is at a loss to know who to select as a groomsman; so Violet asks how Cecil, her old lover, would do. John consents to him if he will accept of the duty. But she is in a quandary as to how he will receive her engagement to John, but, however, she will try and see when all the arrangements are settled.

The carriage is made ready, and Violet and her mother get ready to go home, and Agnes agrees to stay a few days longer. John escorts Violet and her mother to the carriage. They bid the folks good-bye and seat themselves in the carriage. John is going to take them, so as to make still further arrangements. When they get ready to go Agnes again in her glee says, "Good-bye, pets," and then they start for home. They arrive at home about noon, and John puts up his horse until after dinner. He makes the proper arrangements, and they set the wedding day for the second Thursday in June, which would give them two weeks to make ready. John returns home and talks with Agnes about the arrangements which they had made, and requests her to assist Violet to get ready, and she agrees to do so.

Agnes gets ready to go home, and George is sent with her. They are to stop at Violet's on the way and see her about the arrangements with Cecil. He has been over on Sunday evening, and he sees the ring on Violet's finger, and concludes she is engaged. He does not ask her about it, but she, when an opportunity offers, tells him in what high esteem she always held him, and could see no fault in him, but that she was engaged to another who she thought had greater personal charms, and that she still desired his friendship, and that if he would, it was agreeable to have him act as groomsman, by her request. He could not but feel honored, and thanked her, and agreed to her request. She tells him when the wedding will be, and he gets ready to go home, bidding her good night. He goes away with a light heart, but cannot think evil of Violet.

On the next day George and Agnes arrive, and Violet sends John word about what she has done, and it is accepted. Agnes goes on home to prepare for the coming event. Violet is to wear a white silk dress, trimmed in lace, and John is to have a black Prince Albert suit, and the room is to be decorated with beautiful Southern flowers. Cecil is to bring Agnes, who is to be introduced to him by Violet, and

John is to go for Violet himself. It takes a great deal of time to get ready, for there are a great many friends expected, and ample accommodations must be furnished for all.

When the day arrives, the guests have all been invited, and they gather in at the Arno castle to witness the ceremony. The minister is there, and yonder on the hill are two carriages. In the front one are John and Violet and her mother, and behind are Cecil and Agnes. When they arrive they are introduced to the assemblage, and the people vie with each other as to which is the most beautiful couple.

When all is ready they take their places under the large flower arch, John and Cecil on the right, and Violet and Agnes on the left. Then the minister steps forward and says the marriage ceremony in a sweet, audible tone. When the ceremony is over, the people pass around and congratulate the young couple, and wish them a happy life, and the marriage presents are presented to them. Cecil has been as cheerful as anyone, and jestingly remarked: ' I wish it were Agnes and I." Then that wit of Agnes's again flashed forth: "May it be so." But nothing more was thought of it. John and Violet are to occupy the old homestead and see to the estate. The guests return to their homes, speculating on the affair as to the two beautiful couples. Cecil takes Agnes home and leaves an engagement, f r she really is fond of him.

John is now happy with Violet, and wishes to see others happy also. They get Mrs. Payne to agree to live with them, and John sets about improving the estate. There is a great deal more to be done than either John or Violet expected, as they have had litt'e experience in self-sustainance; but they get along very well, for they have studied each other's nature and know full well how to bear and forbear.

Violet is anxious to hear from Agnes and know how she is getting along, so she writes her a letter, telling her how she likes her new home, and how pleasant it is to have a home of her own and to be interested in their own welfare. She likes John's mother very much, for she is a grand old lady, so friendly and sociable. Violet's mother also likes her new home, but cannot forget where she has lived for so many years. She closes by thanking her for past favors.

Agnes is glad to receive this letter from her cousin, and to know that she is so well pleased, and that everything is agreeable to her. Agnes relates that her trip with Cecil was very pleasant, and that he held no envy toward her, and that he considered it an honor to be present at her marriage. Fay missed her friend very much, as they were together a great deal, and were nearly like sisters. She also relates that Cecil made an engagement with her, and that she had formed a good opinion of him, for he was so polite and manly.

John has become more like his father, settled in his habits, and making large gains in his business. John's mother sees that he is successful, and she turns all the estate over to him. Violet is now mistress indeed, and shares in all things. She waits on John's mother with much care, for she is getting very feeble, and she tries to make her last days her best ones.

Cecil has been to see Agnes, and spent a social evening with her. That natural wit makes a cheerful atmosphere to move in, and Cecil found that out at the wedding of John and Violet, when his jest was answered so appropriately. Now, Agnes is not a lady to trifle with one's affections, and then jilt them. She is only a natural humorist, and the flash words ripple off her tongue like water over a pebbly ledge, and are in harmony with the associability of the company. Cecil thinks himself a conquerer to be able to associate with her. His own turn is in that direction—great in the art of entertaining: never at a loss for something to say, and speaks according to ethics. In some this is acquired: in others natural, and is more affable. These twain are natural.

Cecil visits Fay, because she has been so kind to him, and she tells him how lonesome she has been since Violet has been married and gone. He relates to her his acquaintance with Agnes Percy, and asks

her to become acquainted with her, and he calls Agnes
his "funny girl."

Now, Violet was of a still reflective nature, and so
was John Arno. Cecil says he is going over on Sunday afternoon, and asks Fay to go along, and that he
will introduce her to Agnes. When the day comes Fay
is ready and goes with him. Agnes sees them coming
and says to herself, "You'll love your sweetheart,
Cecil." But not so. He explains all to her, and she
is more than pleased that he brought her. The day
is spent in pleasure, and Agnes is queen of the party.
It is a high-spirited company, and Cecil thinks the
flowers are heightened and more beautiful, and that
he himself has more dignity when in her presence
When the day is spent, Cecil leaves a future engagement and bids Agnes good-bye, and the two ladies do
likewise, and Agnes asks Fay to call again. They
are soon on the road home, and conversing on the
events of the day and the pleasures which they had
enjoyed. Fay says: "Cecil, Agnes is a prize, delicate and handsome." Cecil is aware of this, and has
his cap set to win her, but does not let it be known,
and brings everything to bear in that direction. He
knows that she is a cousin of John Arno's, and had
lent her influence to him with Violet. But what of
that? She had a right to; and Agnes knows by Violet
all of Cecil's surroundings, although not acquainted
at that time.

Cecil is buoyed on by her graceful manners, and their frequent meetings ripen into real love. There may be love at first sight, but it requires time to discover the real and natural outpourings of the heart, such as would cause one to cling to another until death would separate them.

Cecil and Agnes make arrangements to pay John and Violet a visit at their new home, and see the beautiful resort, and have a pleasure trip. They are surprised at the castle to see Agnes and Cecil. They did not know they were such good friends, but were glad to see them. John treats Cecil with great respect, which only served to closer attach them as friends. Violet treats Agnes very hospitably, showing her much courtesy, and remarked:

"Who's pets now?"

"Not I," said Agnes; "we're lovers. Are you?"

"Excuse me then, Agnes."

"Certainly, you're excusable."

All this was pleasing conversation between these fast friends. They all take a ramble along the river, and enjoy it very much. Then Cecil and Agnes return home, pleased with their trip, and leave John and Violet to conjecture about them and the outcome of the future.

Their courtship ripens into still closer affections, and Cecil is thinking of asking Agnes for her hand and heart. He knows how lively she is, and he is a little delicate about the way he will do that. It is some worry to him, and he knows how cute and cunning she is, and if not accepted she might reply in a stinging way which would let him down heavy; but then he knows she never tells secrets, and that no one will know what is said. He does not think she might accept in the same manner, but that would be all the more beautiful, and would be cherished as a remembrance of the past, as all such things are but cheerful reflections.

So the court-hip ran along without any more effort of this kind, for it seemed to be a puzzling thing, and Cecil thought nature would provide a way, as it does in everything else, as sometimes thoughtless things are signs or omens of the soul and may be grasped as the truth. "And it may be that I may depend upon this," said Cecil. So he continues spending these social evenings. They walk up and down the road by Mrs. Percy's, until it seems that everything is so familiar that it almost becomes part of their existence. Cecil enjoys this, for he is somewhat of a naturalist and seeks for information, but he never loses his thoughts of Agnes.

Mrs. Percy never troubles herself about her daughter, only that she sees that she does not keep late hours at night, for she thinks that is detrimental to society, as well as bad manners. Cecil is pleased with this, as it has been a part of his culture to observe the rules of etiquette.

As the time whiled by they are seated at the table looking at the ornaments and fancied treasures. It enters Cecil's mind that he will write a few words on a slip of paper which lays on the table near him. He does not deem it necessary to sharpen the pencil, for it is his mental proclivities which are bothering him just now. So he takes the pencil and writes these words:

"I love none other but you."

Then he handed her the paper, and she read it with care: and then she reached for the pencil and just beneath it wrote:

"And that I see."

He then took the pencil and wrote just beneath:

"I will to you be true."

And then she wrote just beneath:

"And I to thee."

Now, collecting these lines, they read as follows:

"I love none other but you."
"And that I see."
"I will to you be true."
"And I to thee."

Now, this was a beautiful verse, meaning a great

deal, but Cecil wished to be certain about its meaning. So he said to Agnes:

"You are a poet. I desired truth, not poetry."

"It expresses both," said Agnes.

And she then discussed poetry as presenting the
true and the beautiful, and that it contained harmony
of thought and harmony of purpose with a sweet,
gentle rhythm, or else there was no poetry, and that
it remained for the poets with the outpourings of the
soul to multiply and magnify the beautiful of earth.
Then he was satisfied that it expressed the feeling of
her heart. And he then raised her left hand and
placed thereon the emblem of their hearts.

Mrs. Percy is consulted, and her consent is obtained; then all is well with Cecil, and they set about
appointing a day and a place for the nuptials. They
settle as to what they will wear, and leave the day
and place for a future time. They think it would be
nice if they could be joined in wedlock at the Arno
castle, and agree to ask John and Violet if it can take
place there. Agnes is to write to them about the
matter, and find out and let Cecil know in time to
make the required arrangements. So Agnes writes
them about it. It is a surprise to them, but it is
agreeable. They are pleased to know that Cecil and
Agnes would select their home for the wedding. They
answer Agnes's letter, and tell her how surprised they
are, and that she and Cecil will be welcome to any-

thing which they can do for them. Agnes conveys
this gratifying news to Cecil, who then goes to see
John, and tells him what he would like to have. John
receives him kindly, and arranges the same room for
the coming event that he had arranged for himself.
Cecil and Agnes will make all the other arrangements and write to the Arnos about it and tell them
the time set for the wedding. John and Violet take
great pains to decorate the rooms beautifully with
flowers and ornaments, and make a large arch of
flowers under which they are to stand. Cecil has
many friends, and all are invited and welcome.

The day set for the marriage is a beautiful one,
and great preparation has been made by Cecil. The
pike leading away from the castle is lined with all
kinds of vehicles. At the appointed hour all is in
readiness, and Cecil and Agnes are coming in a coach,
followed by throngs of people. They arrive and lead
the way to the house over the gravel walk which lies
between two rows of beautiful flower beds, which lend
their sweetness for their happiness. They are ush-
ered into the room prepared for them, and they take
the place assigned to them amidst throngs of people,
and the bridesmaids and groomsmen assume their
duties. When the parties are all ready the minister
is brought in, and he advances quickly to his task of
uniting them by the proper ceremony. The beauty
of the occasion is when they are asked if they take

each other to be husband and wife. The response was low, but it echoed through the room, which caused a solemnity to come over the guests. The couple was beautiful beyond description, and as the guests filed around to congratulate them, you could hear remarks of "beautiful," "grand," "most excellent." Violet had good taste for art, and had done her best in the arrangement of everything, and everything presented perfect harmony. Many gifts were brought for them, and the whole presented one grand appearance. John Arno had not forgotten the kindness of his cousin Agnes, and he presented to her $100 in gold, for which they thanked him very much. The company begin to separate for their homes; and how grand to watch them as they filed away down the pike and out of sight! Could Cecil and Agnes help but be happy when John and Violet had done so much for them? They must be greater friends. The bride and groom are invited to spend the evening at the castle, and they accept. It is the starting of a new life for the young people, and they desired it to be indicative of their future life.

On the morrow they return to Mrs. Percy's and arrange to go to housekeeping. Cecil is a merchant at Queenstown, and does a good business. They take a short trip over to St. Louis and spend a few days in pleasure and sight-seeing. Then Cecil returns to his occupation and purchases a neat resi-

dence, and goes to house-keeping. Never were his
prospects brighter or his life more happy. Agnes is
pleased with her new home, and thinks herself much
exalted by being able to win the heart of such a man.
Agnes soon becomes acquainted with city life, and
likes it very well. Her winning ways and conversation make her a great favorite in city society. Now
Cecil goes about his business with more energy than
ever, for his mind is free and he is contented. His
trade increases, and he accumulates very fast.

Violet writes to Agnes to come over and spend a
few days with her. It has been some time since she
has heard from her. So Agnes gets ready and drives
over to see Violet, for she thinks from the tone of the
letter she is wanted for some express purpose, and
surely it was so, for she wanted to hear from her and
know how she was getting along at Queenstown, for
that was her old home, and she desired to know about
the people and their relation to the world. It is a
nice trip for Agnes, and gives her a little recreation,
relieving her mind from domestic cares. She relates
the comings and goings of her old neighbors, which
is a pleasant relation of circumstances, and that they
have a nice residence on Main street and have it well
furnished. When she gets ready to return home
Violet asks her to come often, and that she will return
the compliment.

Agnes goes back to Queenstown pleased with her

visit, and finds her husband glad to receive her, and he caresses her with the same kindness with which he had always greeted her. Agnes is the same affectionate lady, and her short visit only seemed to cement them more closely together. Cecil thought, as he pillowed his head upon her breast, what a boon it is to have harmony of affections, harmony of love, and the world move on as one harmonious whole. He, with his contented heart, cannot banish from his mind the oft-repeated words that—

"There are as good fish in the sea as was ever caught out."

BESSIE, THE BELLE OF ALAMO.

In a quiet little village,
　　Where sweet flowers bloom and grow,
Roams the fairest of sweet maidens,
　　Christened, the Belle of Alamo.

Always ready with an answer,
　　In a manner mild, but low,
Just becoming of a lady
　　Like the Belle of Alamo.

You can see her at all places,
　　Cheeks quite reddened to a glow,
Modestly bowing to her lovers,
　　Bessie, the Belle of Alamo.

She is cheerful to a pleasure,
　　Where adversities come and go,
Knowing nothing but such kindness
　　Becoming the Belle of Alamo.

She never flirts with transient people,
　　Neither hangs on the gate for show,
But allures by charms so graceful,
　　Bessie, the Belle of Alamo.

You may know her by her beauty,
  Silver tresses hanging low.
Plump in form and mincely stepping,
  This lady, Belle of Alamo.

If you desire to acquaint this lady,
  Watch the lasses where e'er you go;
The mind creates this living beauty.
  Bessie, the Belle of Alamo.

SCENES IN SCHOOL.

As I sat in the halls of learning,
  I cast at the pupils a glare:
Some seemed eager for learning,
  And others were dead to despair;
Some prying over books to gain knowledge,
  And others whose minds are flying around,
Like the wind on the beautiful prairies,
  Carrying vibrations and emotions of sound

Some appear to be created a genius,
  And the world overflows with their care,
While others are debauching their wisdom,
  And lay like a beast in his lair.
But for those who study books carefully
  Are treasures of shining bright gold,
And to those who lounge about idly
  Have ignorance obstructing the soul.

A BIRD'S EYE VIEW OF A COURT ELECTION SCENE.

The great judge sat in his easy chair,
Deciding all laws points legally fair,
Ruling out this and allowing that,
While counsel were playing at tit for tat;
They addressed the court: "May your honor please,"
And some one arose and swayed the breeze.

"I'll state the case," the plaintiff said,
Then from a paper he both spoke and read,
And when there came a little lull,
Defendants were up to plead in full,
And talked at length around about
As to how they thought it would turn out.

The temple of justice was filled to the wall
With shrewd politicians with brass and gall;
There was Tom from the village, Jack from the hills,
And Doc from the office of bottles and squills;
A more motley crowd was never arrayed,
And tactics of schemers were readily displayed.

At every fence-corner and nook in the street
William was intercepted by their wonderful cheek
To hold up the ghost of the shadow of wood,
Which seemed to the defendants to be mighty good;
There was the whisky-dispenser and man with a jag,
And ward politician, the fox for to bag.

There were able attorneys to keep up the fight,
And men who believed in buying outright
A magnetic person that gave no alarm,
A descendant of Adam and boss of a farm,
'Twas said "distributing of dollars in silver at will
To give the old eagle a stamp on the bill."

By all of this rubbish it does now prevail
The rooster was stamped right under the tail,
Except by some persons that plaintiff did meet
In mossy apparel and rags on their feet—
And the poet came in for a share of abuse
By one who had on the head of a goose.

Some men were drowning and grabbing at straws,
Asserting that this and that were the laws,
And drinking of water and striding afar,
Which sounded like the rattle of a trolley street-car;
And this is the way the law mill rolls
When merchandise is made of human souls.

'Tis this woeful shape our country is in,
By talking of tariff and using of tin,
Bordering right closely to darkest Rome,
When people were driven, like a dog with a bone,
By patricians who ruled and wielded all power
And caused the plebeians to yield and to cower.

SIMILE OF GOLD AND SILVER, BY MAID AND MAN.

Man: I reign supreme upon the earth,
        'Twas given me by right of birth
        That I should be the standard power,
        And all beneath should yield their dower.

Maid: Poor thing, what would you be
        If you could not compare with me
        Your fanciful exalted form,
        For which you say that you were born?

Man: I know alone I stood at first,
        No power to replenish sacred earth;
        No one to keep me company,
        To save my schemes from eternity.

Maid: I thought you'd see that to the strong
        A helpmate most surely does belong.
        Partaking of the self-same right,
        Stamped by the ancient original fiat.

Man: But is there no distinction, none,
        To this the first-created one:
        Who first set foot upon this sward,
        The image of the eternal Lord?

Maid: No, there's no distinction, not a bit,
        So says the sacred holy writ;
        The covenant says they two are twain
        From antiquity to end of reign.

Man: There's no escape from this combination
     thread
     Upon which is based the goddess of liberty's
     head,
     That in the balance they lie side by side,
     To stay the wheels of the flowing tide.

Maid: Whose issue is this to be,
     Circulating from sea to sea?
     Is it not based upon these two,
     Which carries this co-ordination through?

Man: I must acknowledge that in the end
     That each the other's rights defend;
     And this is surely the very goal
     Upon whose issue rests the whole.

Maid: So parity is an idle thought
     As compared to things which God hath
     wrought:
     No more we'll hear of co-operative money
     at par,
     But the rattling wheels of the commercial car.

Man: This offspring jointly we must bear,
     Chased around the world to the teller's bar;
     It seems to me to the pageant this is fair
     To adjust this wheel of fortune right with
     care;
     Or in other words, I trow, would be the plan,
     To adjust it equal, like maid and man.

THE WRECKED TRAIN.

We boarded the train on the Northern Pacific,
The mountain scenery was grand and prolific,
To make a through trip to the end of the line,
Although in December the weather was fine;
The passengers were quite cheerful and laughing
As the wheels on the rails to powder were chaffing.

It was a gala day in old Vancouver's Isle,
All faces aglow with a pleasant smile.
When all are on board a whistle to start,
And soon dearest friends are distant apart;
We passed through the valley and saw the white plain.
Our engine did rally through snow and through rain.

We're approaching the mountain and see the white
        dome,
There's a beautiful fountain runs down thro' the bone.
On nearing the summit there's a whistle for brakes.
As she starts like a plummet and everything shakes.
To pass over the canyon and down the east slope,
The passengers are crying, O God, the trestle's broke!

The coaches are falling and swinging in air,
The passengers are wringing their hands in despair;
But the engine is pulling with all of her might
While the coaches are swinging, O heaven, such a sight!
The coupling is holding the cars like a leech,
Suspended in air like a kite on the beach.

Two coaches are swinging in the chasm below,
And with the sway of the wind they move to and fro,
While the train hands are scaffolding the people to
    save
From a horrible death which ends in the grave,
The conductor looked out and loudly did call:
"Oh, hurry up, boys, I fear she will fall;

Go bring on the timbers and lay them across,"
And most of the time we worked at a loss;
Our eyes on the coaches that's swinging o'er head,
Our veins are all swollen and faces are red;
We heave up the timbers without scaffold or sweep
Until the rude structure the danger line meets.

When we climb to the coaches with chisel and sledge
And beat on the doors like beating a wedge,
The door is broken open, we see them fall out
As if they were half dead and moping about;
But no one is hurt, not even a scar
Is left on their foreheads to show they fell far.

When the cars are all empty we sever their ties,
She's dashed into pieces, in splinters she lies;
Then the train moved forward to a place in the road
To receive the bold rescuers and unfortunate load.
There's a signal for starting, the smoke's rolling high,
We're again on our journey. Old trestle, good-bye!

ALAMO.

When I was young and full of glee,
And apt to wander around
Like many a boy I wanted to see
A little country town.
And to a place I longed to go
Whose name was christened Alamo.

It was a place to me quite rare,
On going with my father there,
As oft as I could plead with him
To please and let me go again.
And thus, you see, I learned to know
The road which led to Alamo.

And then I became an errand boy,
Buying things, which was great joy,
Coming forth with home again,
Better than the grown-up men,
Which made my mind so richly glow
With all the scenes in Alamo.

So well I remember the graded school,
Where often we did break the rules,
And gave the teachers lots to do
In dealing with their motley crew.
To make us learn that we might show
There were great men in Alamo.

There were three churches in the place,
Where we might grow in knowledge and grace,
And worship according to our will
The God who gave us all our skill;
And long we've wandered to and fro
To behold the town of Alamo.

Of a Sunday the bells did chime,
Calling the children from every clime
To come and learn a blessed thing
Of our dear Savior's suffering.
That we be ready when we go
To leave in death dear Alamo.

And now we're grown to aged men,
Scattered all over glade and glen;
Some are lawyers, great and smart,
Some are preachers to the heart.
Some are teachers, not a few,
Some are farmers, pure and true.

And so you see how riches flow
Through the portals of Alamo.
And in the cemetery, east of town,
Many a classmate may be found
Which has fallen by the grace of Him
Who can pardon every sin;

But He's called them when pure and right
For to take their upward flight,
To meet in heaven far above,
Where all is pure and God is love.
And so I hope that time may show
We may all meet again from Alamo.

THE GERM OR NUCLEUS OF ALAMO.

Amidst forests and vines of a golden hue
  A mixed population co-mingled;
They tugged and hauled their baggage through,
  And lived in huts board-shingled.

A string and a latch was the bolt of the door,
  Which was made of oaken slab puncheon,
While the earth or rude timbers served as a floor,
  And corn bread with dried venison made them a
    luncheon.

But the woods disappeared before the strong arms,
  As the strokes of the axmen were falling.
And thus there appeared these beautiful farms,
  An honor to those of their calling.

But they needed a town where they could go
  And buy of those things mostly needed,
So Samuel Truax and William Boice christened our
    Alamo,
  A beautiful place, now conceded.

In honor of Davy Crockett our town was so named,
　Who poured out his life's blood when old and quite
　　boary;
As a gallant swordsman he'll always be famed;
　Like all of our heroes, he stood for Old Glory.

GERM OR NUCLEUS OF ALAMO.

A school house was built of chinken and logs,
　Where pedagogues stalked, beat and pounded;
No studying nature or peat of the bogs,
　But the old rule of three must be expounded.

Those days are all o'er of fireside lore,
    And tales of escapes bold and daring:
Those primeval times will be never more,
    Nor the bright shining light of the clearing.

A new epoch has come with learning and art,
    With this structure of wisdom, fine, large and hand-
        some:
It is the soul's pride of every pure heart,
    For learning is free without ransom.

The old pedagogue, with his rod and his rule,
    Is a thing of the past forever and ever:
An up-to-date Prof. will fill our new school,
    Teaching wisdom and languages stylish and clever.

But the quaint old bell in its new tower exists—
    Its peals are loud and sonorous:
It breaks the sad heart of some pessimists,
    But joyful is the youth now before us.

The poor wooden structure, with windows of gauze,
    Is displaced by new ones of glass:
To enlighten the children has been the whole cause,
    And the door-latch of wood is now brass.

The entering steps, where oft children played,
    Are now made of long slabs of stone:
It isn't the place where we loitered and stayed
    When dismissed from our school to go home.

And the chopping of wood by the elderly boys
　To keep out the cold, chilly air,
Is now done away in comfort and joys
　In an edifice all heated with care.

But great men have arisen e'en all of this,
　And have filled many places of trust.
And more of like calling will not go amiss
　If they but brighten and polish the rust.

Let us cherish the good and enlighten the soul,
　And build up a place famed for its grandeur;
There is no other way of attaining the goal
　In that hoped-for beyond in its splendor.

THE CRICKET.

Under every bark and litter
You can hear the little critter
All the dark night long.
Singing his busy song—
　　　　　K-e-r-t!　K-e-r-t!

In the musty wheat shock,
And under every little rock,
The silence is invariably broken
By the notes that are spoken—
　　　　　K-e-r-t!　K-e-r-t!

In the mouldering clothes case
And the old-fa-hioned fireplace.
You can hear his little notes
As from his lips it floats—
                    K-e-r-t!   K-e-r-t!

All among your Sunday clothes
You will find his dainty nose,
Looking where to take his toll,
And now and then he makes a hole.
                    K-e-r-t!   K-e-r-t!

In among the apples mellow
You will find this noisy fellow,
As he bites the apple peel
For to make his dainty meal—
                    K-e-r-t!   K-e-r-t!

All among the logs and moss
You can hear the little boss,
And everything where e'er you pass.
Even in the dewy grass —
                    K-e-r-t!   K-e-r-t!

HEROES OF SANTIAGO DE CUBA.

Sampson's fleet stood out at sea,
    Guarding Santiago bay.
The Stars and Stripes waved o'er it free,
    While Cervera hidden lay.

To catch the Spanish in a trap
    Was planned by Hobson's braves;
The Merrimac was chose for that—
    She plowed the billowy waves.

With seven seamen she sped in port,
    To quaint old Morro's walls;
The Dons stood silent in the fort,
    Aghast at the captain's calls.

They faced the shot and shell on shore,
    And reached the place designed.
Amidst the cannons' deafening roar
    And subterranean mines.

The ensign o'er the collier's deck
    Said, "Liberty, ye Cuban braves!"
When purposely the ship was wrecked,
    And the world looked on amazed.

Oh! our heroes, where are they
    That took the hazard risk?
We see them through the darkened spray,
    Hurrah! hurrah! to shore they drift.

The Spanish captors are near to them,
    A shout of deafening roar;
Hispani ne'er has seen such men
    Since Horatius, long before,

The thing is done.   Cervera's fate
    Will tell Alphonso's woe.
While Sampson holds the bottled fleet,
    Our Miles will charge the foe.

The end is near, and Spanish reign,
    With blood and stench and crime,
Will be avenged for the battle Maine
    Forever and all time.

INDIANA.

On the plains of Indiana,
    Where the wild flowers gently wave,
There the farmers in their splendor
    Do the golden cereals raise.
There is lands of various dimensions,
    From the valleys to the hills,
Many streams that are rippling.
    Near by which we build our mills.

We have prairies, we have woodlands,
    Richest treasures ever stored;
And far down in the interior
    Natural gas we have in hoard—
Quite enough to run our factories
    Just as long as wheels may roll,
And as you are nearing Anderson,
    There's the richest of the goal.

Through the center runs the Wabash,
  With its rich alluvial soil:
From its source unto its ending
  Many sturdy farmers toil,
Not alone with bone and sinew,
  But a little more at ease,
Like unto our honored statesman,
  Whose giant speeches always please.

This is not all that I can tell you:
  We're the gateway to the West,
And must be crossed by many tourists
  Hunting places where to rest
From the cares and toils of business,
  Which they've followed many a year,
Storing up a little fortune
  For old age and later cares.

SHOE COBBLER.

The cobbler sits on his leather stool,
  And thongs the best he can;
He blows his horn and turns about,
  And chafes the end of man.

He is a perfect weather-cock,
  And can tell the wind and time;
He pounds away on flattening-rock,
  And spends his force of mind.

6

He sits amidst old rancid shoes—
  A splendid scent and savor;
'Twould give an epicure the blues
  To smell this foot-made flavor.

When his race is run and he is done
  A-mending of old soles,
He's laid away for another day—
  A subject for the ghouls.

THE SOUL.

The soul is immortal, we cannot tell why,
Unless it has come from God in the sky.
In death it is separated from this body of ours,
To go to its keeper in a mansion of towers,
Where all on a level will soar without wings,
To dwell in a city—a kingdom of kings.
The wheat is separated away from the chaff,
While the wicked are left to mock and quaff.

We images will be in our bodily form,
Preserving identity, although newly born.
The power of communion invested in we,
Conversing with brothers we've longed to see.
We'll meet those old martyrs, gone long before
To dwell with their Savior, and open the door
For the sheep of the shepherd who have striven in vain
To reach those green pastures where purity reigns.

A description of heaven was given to thee
By St. John on the Patmos, an isle of the sea.
He saw the rich treasures and emerald stone,
The mantling robes around the great throne,
With Christ there ascended his people to descry,
Discerning their actions, to judge by and by.

THE SHADES.

Oh! come to the Shades, ye wandering tourists,
    There beautiful scenery your eyes to behold,
From its beautiful waters, its green-growing shrub'ry,
    To its rock-bound clifts which enlighten the soul.
Oh! come to me now, while my buds are all bursting.
    Their sweet-smelling odor with the air to diffuse;
I'll fill your hearts gladly with all that grows wildly—
    The old and the young I readily amuse.

Come to me, ye loved ones, whose minds are all bur-
        dened
    With the cares of a life's oppressions and toils,
And I'll give you a field of fun and of pleasure
    To banish your minds from remorse and from broils.
I am glowing with verdure from valley to summit,
    Whose blossoms of beauty are growing all wild,
Which calls back the aged one from the time of their
        manhood
    To their earlier days, when they were a child.

I'm a place for those people whose banks have made
    failures,
  And want to get away from the cares of their home;
They can bring out their lasses and fish for the basses,
  And promenade proudly the Devil's Backbone.

THE SHADES.

This great massive structure is nature's own handwork:
  Two high solid walls, sixty feet in mid-air,
Four feet in its thickness, connecting two ridges—
  There's nothing so grand that we can compare.

The fowls of the heavens make nests in the burrows,
  Which God has ordained, the rocks being loose:
The pine and the spruce, looking down on the billows,
  Has given its name: the old Buzzard Roost.
A lady once fell from this high-towering precipice—
  Her mind seemed to float with the calm gentle breeze:
She toppled right over, as if to destruction,
  And was barely saved by the boughs of some trees.

Near the mouth of Little Ranty is picturesque falls,
  The most beautiful of all cascades;
An old-time stair leads up the great walls.
  As you pass through the flume to the Shades
The waters are scattered in fan-like rays,
  As they strand o'er the round-like dome,
And dashing down in silver spray,
  They rush on in biliows of foam.

JUGGING BUMBLEBEES.

Little Clarence went to the meadow
  To play on the new-mown hay,
Where a bumblebee got after him
  And run him clear away.
He told his mamma about the bees
  And all that they had done,
Then hunted up a water jug
  And said he'd have some fun.

He filled it partly with water,
　It made a roaring sound,
Then placed the jug quite near the nest
　When none of them were 'round.
He then procured a little stick
　And gave the ground a thug:
They all came out and flew around
　And sailed right in the jug.

When they were in the water deep
　And drowned, which seemed quite funny,
He hunted up the little nest
　And took their bread and honey.
Thus we see by cunning device
　We can such things entwine,
But yet it seems so very nice
　To treat them so unkind:
For we do dread their mighty sting,
　It appears so very sharp.
And hurts much worse than anything—
　It pierces to our heart.

Come all you boys and learn of me,
　And you can have some pleasure:
When you have nothing else to do
　But spend your time at leisure,
And get a jug with water in,
　Which makes a noise like singing,

And you can take the bees right in
  Without the fear of stinging;
Then when you see the coast is clear,
  And they have gone to rest,
You can come up without much fear
And procure their cozy nest.

WORKINGS OF BEES.

Little bees are flying high—
When the day is fair and dry
Humming are his little wings,
You can hear him as he sings,
Carrying home his little sweets
In his pouch or on his feet.

On rich blossoms he does glide,
Turning quick from side to side,
Hunting for the sweetest cups,
Out of which he takes his sups,
Until he has made his round,
Then you see him homeward bound.

In his hive you'll find his cells,
Which are numerous honey wells,
Flowing richly to the top
In his luxurious honey crop,
Which he's laid by with those wings
To save his life until the spring.

As soon as spring and it is warm,
You can see them by the swarm
Working hard for sixty days—
The life of bees in working phase—
But younger ones are coming on
Long before the old are gone.

In their hive you'll find a cup
Shaped just like a hickory nut:
In this place the old queen plays.
And passing round the eggs she lays
For the increasing of the bees
When the old are at their ease.

RAISING THE FLAG.

Who will raise the grand old flag
    O'er a desolate Spanish realm,
And life and liberty guarantee
    Where murder guides the helm?
Why! the Union boys in blue
    Will sacrifice the last drop of blood
To the cause of liberty true—
    Will expel a tyrant lord.

Who will set the reconcentradoes free
    From their shackles and iron bands,
Where Columbus on his bended knee
    Prayed the God of Christian lands?

Why! the Union boys in blue,
    With the cross of Christ on high,
Have heard of pitiful slaves pierced through,
    And have rallied to the battle cry.

Who will liberate the poor and oppressed,
    As they toil without food for the crown,
Penniless, wan, emaciated, distressed,
    No bed for repose but the ground?
Why! the Union boys in blue
    Will go like a hero to the strife,
And strain every muscle anew
    For a nation that struggles for life.

We come not like a conquering foe,
    For power and pelf and lands;
But, innocent as the mountain roe,
    With amity and outstretched hands,
Go build for yourselves a state,
    Let "Libre" be written to tell
How ye fought with tyrant strong and great—
    How the enemy ye did expel.

"Go free, dear Cuba," says the flag,
    As it waves o'er El Caney's crest.
"You've trod the Spanish winepress in rags,
    But your oppressors have done gone to rest."
"Go free," says the gallant Rough Riders,
    As they sally away from the port,
And are driving the renegade Spanish
    Inside of old Morro Fort.

"Go free! dearest Isles of the Indies;
   For centuries you've been trodden down;,
Cry Libre! Libre! Libre!
   You're forever free from a crown.
Make for yourselves a government,
   While we guide, assist and protect;
Place a star in the field of your emblem,
   That you meditate, think and reflect."

Old Liberty Bell rung not in vain,
   Our Declaration says just what it means:
We'll extend a blessing under oppression's reign
   To the ancient Isles of the Philippines.
Go teach the Gospel in foreign lands,
   Give them a hope, a faith in Him;
Extend God's grace, ye Christian bands:
   Teach them the power to pardon sin.

Let us succor the innocent mongrel child—
   A noble spirit may dwell within:
In their humble state in the jungles wild
   A nomadic tale their life has been.
Their masters coveted only spoil—
   No builders of the inward man,
But day by day incessant toil
   For Spanish friars—a Corsair clan.

Think not of trade or commercial power,
   But hold the lives of a people dear;
Go give to them a better dower,
   And of our freedom let them hear.

Oppress them not; be merciful and kind;
  Let them absorb our modern ways,
Until they see, or some way find,
  Their change of life is better days.

CHILDISH GLEE.

They gambol in the sunshine,
  Through the woods and dells;
As it's nearing noontime
  They're resting at the well.

Gathering velvet mosses
  From the rocks and rills,
Making pretty flosses,
  Scampering over hills.

Strolling by the brooklets,
  Pebbles shining bright,
There is joy in every nooklet,
  Gems like stars of night.

Murmuring are the waters
  As they ripple down;
Bark boats of tiny squatters
  Pass by from fairy town.

Birds are singing sweetly
  Among the leafy trees;
Everything is lovely,
  Sweet-scented is the breeze.

They have ruddy little faces,
    Made so by the sun:
Running and skipping races—
    Jolly childish fun.

CHILDISH GLEE

There is music in the foliage,
    Tunes of nature's art,—
Enlightening the little sages,
    And soothing the childish heart.

Waves of sward like ocean,
    Nodding is the grain.
Everything in motion,
    Dropping is the rain.

*Toad-stools are a-ticking
  Like our father's clock;
Thorns for pins are sticking
  In the baby's frock.

Mosses for the carpets,
  On the ground-made floor;
Many colored leaflets
  Strewn about the door.

Now mamma is calling,
  As they pluck a rose;
Hear them all applauding,
  As the scene must close.

A BACK-WOODS SCHOOL.

The old-time school has had its knell,
And all those noisy feet we used to quell,
Turning slates and leafing books,
Full of mischief turns and crooks.
You could see their faces flow
With the mischief all aglow;
Eyes on teacher, never fail
For to think of water pail:
And when the teacher's back was turned
They would forget quite all they'd learned.

* By Toad-stools is meant Polyporus versicolor. It grows on decaying trees like a half moon, with a white face and a brown one, and looks like the face of a clock. Children use them as clocks.

Some threw wads across the room,
And if the teacher turned too soon
They studied lessons with a rush,
Cheeks all reddened to a blush—
Innocent, we knew full well,
For ne'er a one the tale could tell.
Then the case it rested so,
For the proof fell far below;
But the teacher assured them it would not do
To repeat it, if he got a clew,
Or he would punish to the law
With a gad that's green and raw.

ALONE IN THE WOODS.

As I sat beneath the azure sky,
    The sun beamed warm and pleasant;
There was not a rustle or a cry.
    But the whirring of the pheasant.

The shady dells were like a dream
    Enchanted by the song-birds;
A paradise it almost seemed,
    With pleasures passing by myriads.

I felt myself in Fairy Land,
    With scarce the power of moving—
As happy as a seraph band
    Around the throne hallooing.

In these glens of sweetest music,
    What is life to you or me,
But beholding of those pleasures
    One would fairly wish to see?

Pictures of the living present,
    Fanciful beyond all art,
Richest of all earthly treasures,
    Settled deep within our hearts.

And as the sun is setting, going,
    Darker shades are drawing nigh;
Then will come an electric showing,
    Mirrored on the western sky.

Streamers of a golden twilight,
    Emblems of a dying day--
Scenes which follow brightest sunshine,
    As its rays are drawn away.

YOUNTSVILLE.

On an eastern slope, where shines the sun,
A village long time ago begun;
A blacksmith shop, a grinding and woolen mill,
Were just beneath the little hill;
But now a new impetus brings
A graded school with drooping wings,

With Finks and Snyders, O'Neals, too,
'Tis hard to tell you how it grew;
But there has been no want of skill
In the little hamlet of Yountsville,
And every wave some intelligence brings
From the belfry tower with drooping wings.

The master builder was a man of power,
He built an edifice with gilded tower,
Immersed in wisdom deep at heart
That learning to the soul embark:
And to the children this building flings
Good tidings from those drooping wings.

This stately mansion is grand, indeed,
'Tis gleaning chaff from among the weeds;
It quickens life unto the soul,
It is a boon in deepest goal
And to its hall the urchin brings,
Beneath the belfry with drooping wings.

The bell peals out from its high-up perch,
Excelling that of the village church,
Calling the children to fall in line
And learn a lesson of the Sacred Shrine.
This, I tell you, is just the thing
Which issues from those drooping wings.

The Old Oaken Bucket is far surpassed—
We've piped the earth for deeper gas;
This is a child of recent skill;
No water wheel, no water mill,
But steam that's gushing from iron rings,
Is just beneath those drooping wings.

Now, of these things I speak in praise—
I do approve of modern ways.
Train up your sons like stately men,
To be an honor to all their ken;
And of your town don't fail to sing,
And the grandeur of those drooping wings.

A DESCRIPTION OF HISTORY.

In the life of a nation, accounts must be kept,
  To enlighten a people coming after;
If it wasn't for this events would have slept,
  And weakened our store of good treasure.

But, luckily, man like a genius has been,
  In recording those things which were passing,
Until we have pages from stylus and pen,
  With the many events that's amassing.

On this river of time we have handed down
  All that is grand of a nation;
We can now behold from clay tablets of old
  All Christendom clear down to creation.

Our mind is like a vessel laden with fruit
  That grew over a far distant ocean,
But it is ripening now with each turn of the plow,
  Which quicken our pages in motion.

In a picture of thought we see many things
  Which the chroniclers have penned for their glory:
And we children of skill can read with a will
  The deeds of a people grown hoary.

There's profit by those who have gone on before,
  And have mirrored their thoughts by the pages:
It is better than gold or gems that are old,
  Which must shine out and glitter for ages.

THE OLD SAWMILL.

Toot! toot! toot!   The time has come
When sawmill labor has begun.
Roll on the log and dog it down,
And turn the adjusting lever 'round;
Turn on the steam and let her go:
The dust is flying like the snow!

Reverse the lever, it will stop,
And on a car the plank will drop.
There is a man that's standing there
To seize the planks and off-bear:
They take them to the edging saw,
And then you'll hear a buzzing yaw.

The fireman gathers up the scraps,
And in the fiery furnace slaps,
The blaze goes curling through the flue;
The saw is like a brilliant blue,
And when the mill is running right
The saw is clearly out of sight!

Busy hands are at the mill,
For every man has a place to fill;
And if you stand and gaze around,
A loosened bark will hit your crown,
And on your nose or forehead lodge—
And when too late you're sure to dodge.

ALCOHOL.

Alcohol is like a snake:
    It can't be kept in bounds;
It makes of one a perfect wreck,
    A wandering vagrant hound.

It steals away an active brain,
    And fills one with remorse,
And causes people to go insane,
    Their soul is all morose.

In dread of those, we stand in awe,
    Who tipple at the wine;
They all disgrace the moral laws—
    Their manners are unkind.

All sons and daughters should abhor
  The actions of such loots—
For this is what they make themselves
  When whisky's up their snoots.

Of all the curses on the earth,
  This certainly is the worst;
It brings to sadness and to gloom
  Our pleasures and our mirth.

And he who drinks the fiery cup
  Will come to saddest woes,
For, as he takes each dainty sup,
  'Twill blossom on his nose.

OVER THE HILLS TO THE SCHOOL HOUSE.

Over the hills to the school house
  The teacher is plodding his way,
To instruct those frolicsome urchins
  Who, like snowbirds, are busy at play.

His duties are many and kindred
  To those of a parent at home—
So loving, so gentle and child-like
  He must treat each pupil that comes.

Their faces are shining with gladness
  To see the first sprinkle of snow;
Then off with their wraps and sleigh-bobs
  To coast down the hill they will go.

When the sun is melting the snow-drifts,
  They'll be rolling it up with their hands,
And shaping it into a rock cliff,
  Or making it into a man.

Then they'll choose sides for a battle,
  The enemy a large heap of snow;
They distance themselves from the target—
  One, two, make ready to throw!

The mummy is shattered asunder,
  Sharp-shooters are trying their guns;
Now the teacher is pulling the bell-rope,
  And away goes sweetcake and buns.

They settle themselves in their places.
  And commence humming like numerous bees,
Perusing their books to learn wisdom,
  All leafing and turning the leaves.

Class number one has its lesson.
  And the master calls it on time;
At a tap of the bell they are standing,
  And two taps, they are falling in line.

"Now, Johnnie, you answer the question
  That I have propounded to you:"
A similar routine in connection,
  And the day's recitations are through.

Then they return to their threshold,
  Their prayers are quietly said,
And now they are donning their night clothes,
  And mamma will put them to bed.

CRAWFORDSVILLE, ALIAS ATHENE.

The city of Crawford is a beautiful town.
Where knowledge and learning doth abound,
    In the great theatrical arena;
It is a place that has much fame,
And transient people are gently tame
    When in the city of Athene.

Our modern people have pluck and skill,
They push right onward up the hill,
    Where natural science is gleamy;
And yet they associate the whole
And give to physics a perfect soul,
    These wily students of Athene.

Commerce is pressing in every nook,
The old landmarks they have forsook,
    And all that's dark and dreamy;
Nothing assumes a haggard look,
And life is like a sparkling brook
    In this bustling city of Athene.

We are marching onward with the tide,
Around the world we swiftly glide,
　　The future looks bright and beamy;
The laggard is dropping out behind,
Although their friends are true and kind
　　In the ever-aspiring Athene.

We cannot stay this business roil,
While pressing onward to reach the goal
　　In this philosophical arena;
We are pushing on toward the skies
To meet the patriarchs, so wise—
　　Our people of great Athene.

The annals of time will tell our fate,
And of our people growing great
　　In our city with such vehemy;*
Our fame is laureled in ev'ry clime,
And history impressed on the wings of time,
　　Of our people of great Athene.

THE RED BIRD.

The red bird sat upon a tree,
And sang to me, and sang to me.
The sweetness of his voice did float
From the airy waves of his little throat.

---

* This word is coined from vehemence.

The tune that he sang pierced to my heart,
Exciting a love that ne'er will part
For the little singer so full of glee
And the melodious notes from the old elm tree.

THE RED BIRD.

But still it seemed that he would not tire,
As he mounted up still higher and higher,
And warbled a lay I ne'er have heard
From the sweetest voice of a singing bird.

The morning came, and soon was spent;
The sun to the topmost sky had sent
His brilliant rays to light the earth
And the beautiful morning which it gave birth.

His glee extended to the hour of eight,
When the time of feeding was getting late,
And the young ones croaked for a dainty meal,
A worm or a bug from the new-plowed field.

Then the mock-bird thought he'd imitate,
But fell far short in his self-conceit.
His dress apparel weren't near so red,
And the whitting song was stale and dead.

But yet, as eager as pride could be,
He sang away with his rhythm, to-ree!
Until the flowers with shame did blush,
Which caused his mimicry soon to hush.

But on went the warbler with lay so sweet,
That it savored the morsels the little ones eat,
And taught them a lesson which all should know:
That the way to be happy is to try to be so.

SOLDIERS' MONUMENT.

Our soldiers fought and bled and died
　　The Stars and Stripes to maintain;
A monument will be their pride
　　To speak aloud their fame.

They left their wives and families dear
　To face the maddened foe;
Some ne'er came back is very clear—
　Their bodies lie cold below.

But in our minds, so calm and bright,
　This pedestal stands aloft;
It sheds a lustre of passing light—
　Their memories can't be lost.

And to those children which are bereaved,
　This statue does proclaim,
In honor of our country
　Their fathers have been slain.

That we acknowledge their sacrifice,
　And must the deed repay,
This is an emblem of our love,
　In honor of the fray.

They chased the enemy on battlefields,
　Like chieftains would a knave,
And to the people did reveal
　The grand old flag must wave.

Their families dear are in our hearts,
　We all must care for them;
The government has set apart
　Emoluments for the men.

But those who died in the battle's rage,
  No tithes can they receive
But by an ensign for every age,
  Which speaks in lasting praise.

And on its sides we must inscribe
  The grandest names of yore,
So passing people may imbibe
  Their deeds forever more.

OFFICE-SEEKING.

The rush for office is quite free,
  And candidates are plenty;
It's just because there's no money—
  Their pocket-books are empty.

Uncle Sam has lured us so,
  In taking by taxation,
From off the farm we're forced to go,
  We cannot make connection.

A mortgage on a horse or cow
  Isn't worth the holding;
How can a man support a frow
  Unless by office-holding?

Our wheat is worth but sixty cents,
  And beef not worth a penny;
This is the reason, in common sense,
  That candidates are many.

CHILDHOOD IN THE ORCHARD.

Grand was the scene before us,
　With Junes and Rhode Island green,
Where fathers used to scold us
　For knocking the Summer Queens.

That striped fruit we cherished
　And gathered with a will,
Our little bodies nourished,
　From fruits off of the hill.

Here passed the best of childhood,
　Climbing in the trees:
'Twas equal to the wild-wood,
　With flowers and scented breeze.

We long to be a child again,
　And live a hermit life,
Away from all the cares of men,
　Where youthful pleasure's rife.

Where childhood is a springtime,
　Ripening in the sun,
Like the flowers of ages,
　And life is full of fun.

Those precious golden moments,
　Spent in loving childish mirth,
Is the sweetest of a lifetime,
　Gathering fruits from flowers of earth.

Fruits we cannot carry with us,
  To a land of sweet repose;
But by our fruits the people know us,
  As they know the sweetest rose.

THE HERO OF MANILA.

Of all the men that sail o'er the seas,
  And are standing for Old Glory,
There's none so brave and at their ease
  As George Dewey, old and hoary.
He has plowed the billows and the waves,
  Which ran 'most mountain high;
His name is laureled with the braves,
  His fame—'twill never die.
Hoist all the flags and fire the guns,
  Our hero is not alone;
Ring out, wild bells, your echoes tell
  George Dewey is coming home!

A message flashed across the sea:
  "Protect your native land!"
He received it with such cheer and glee,
  And sailed for Manila strand.
The Spanish guns along the way
  Belched forth a deafening roar;
The admiral's words were calm that day,
  As down on the enemy he bore.

Hoist all the flags and fire the guns,
  Our hero is not alone:
Ring out, wild bells, your echoes tell
  George Dewey is coming home!

He passed the entrance of the bay,
  O'er magazines and mines;
Our seamen won in every fray,
  And beat them every time.
Brave Dewey signalled from the deck
  To fire on the Spanish knaves,
And soon we saw their ships a-wreck,
  And floating on the waves.
Hoist all the flags and fire the guns,
  Our hero is not alone:
Ring out, wild bells, your echoes tell
  George Dewey is coming home!

The work is done, the flag is raised
  Amidst the battle's cry:
The boys in blue must all be praised—
  They mean to do or die.
Manila is ours by right of war,
  We'll treat the people kind;
This sheer oppression we abhor—
  No truer friend they'll find.
Hoist all the flags and fire the guns,
  Our hero is not alone;
Ring out, wild bells, your echoes tell
  George Dewey is coming home!

The victor starts out to retrace
  His course across the sea:
A perfect type of the American race—
  A friend to you and me.
He meets the kings along the route,
  And feasts with noble queens;
We hear the guns and people shout,
  And martial music teems.
Hoist all the flags and fire the guns,
  Our hero is not alone;
Ring out, wild bells, your echoes tell
  George Dewey has come home!

THE SAVIOR.

It was in good old Bethlehem,
  Where the fairest baby lay,
In the rudest of a manger,
  On swaddling cloths and hay.

'Twas on a lonely evening
  That the people's fate was sealed
With a promise of redemption,
  And eternal life revealed.

A star shone in the heavens
  Above where the Savior lay:
A light to those in darkness
  To guide them on their way.

And lo! the shepherds saw it
  While attending to their sheep,
And, rushing onward to it,
  They found the child asleep.

The time was so exciting,
  And the kings were all beguiled.
As they sought with such impatience
  The life of the infant child.

But day by day he was growing
  In knowledge and in grace:
Ordained the soul-redeemer
  Of all the human race.

When he reached his manhood,
  He perfected His plan,
By dying on the cross-tree
  At the wicked hands of man.

His soul ascended upward,
  And his body to the tomb;
The day was clothed in darkness
  And the earth was all in gloom

He now is with the Father,
  And is sitting on the throne,
Awaiting of the judgment
  To call His people home.

THE EDITORS.

The editors are a jolly lot,
  And yet they feel quite mellow:
They fill their sheets with much that's not
  So pleasant to the other fellow.

They talk at length, and to the point,
  And always get so giddy
You'd think their pen was out of joint,
  Like the tongue of an Irish biddy.

And yet they feel as safe as mice
  Hid in some dusky barracks,
Awaiting for to break the ice
  From some lucid son of Garrick's.

Sometimes they meet upon the street
  Some lady filled with pride:
We then do hear some shuffling feet
  And twirling of rawhide.

Away they go up Lundy's lane,
  The editor much in the lead:
The damsel followed by her train,
  Attached to her raging steed.

Next issue then will be explained,
  And both be satisfied:
The censure shows they both are blamed,
  And both have lost some pride.

8

And thus they go from year to year,
   Exposing by the legions,
And reaching out, both far and near,
   Through all the world and regions.

ELECTION DAY.

Election day is coming, with all that pomp can wield:
Electors are protected by an artificial shield.
Boodlers have defrauded this sacred trust of men,
Until we have devised a plan with stall and chute for
      them;
A die that stamps the chosen one, a juror in the box,
They there receive no emoluments, and cheat the sly
      old fox,
By passing in behind the screen, away from longing eyes,
And fixing out their ballots, concealed from those that
      buys.
This ballot must be counted according to the mark
That's placed thereon, without restraint, the symbol
      of their heart.
Then hand the stamp to the polling clerk, the ticket
      to inspector,
Go on your way rejoicing then, your conscience clear
      as nectar.
Schemes and fraud are dormant now, the people have
      ascended;
No more they'll milk the fatted cow, our rights are
      strongly blended.

The milk will flow the other way, there's crystals in
    the butter;
We are so glad we're free again, our hearts doth fairly
    flutter.
The ship of state will still sail on, the sea is calm and
    easy;
The schemers' cry is passing by, their mantle's dark
    and greasy.

LITTLE DOG FRED.

I have a little dog whose name is Fred,
    He runs with me to play;
He has four eyes within his head—
    Two bright, two dim were they.

He has four feet that's colored tan,
    And he frolics on the hay;
You'd think he was a little man—
    He walked upright to-day.

I'll hold some food above his head,
    Poor fellow, he will speak;
He always does so when he's fed,
    When things are out his reach.

He chases the rabbits in the woods,
    And the squirrels up the trees;
He watches the chickens with their broods,
    And snaps the bumblebees.

He has a coat as black as jet,
  And teeth as white as snow;
He is the very nicest pet
  That one can ever know.

LITTLE DOG FRED.

He carries sticks along the road,
  And trots along to school;
The teacher never needs a goad,
  For he doesn't break the rules.

He scours the pastures for the cows,
And does not fear to roam:
He never stops his bow-wow-wows
Until he brings them home.

A SNOWFLAKE.

Whenever a snowflake leaves the sky,
It turns and turns around to sigh:
"Good-bye, dear mother in vaulted blue,
Some day again I'll come to you—
Not in crystals frozen white,
But in liquid prisms bright:
Amidst fervent heat I'll take new wings,
While gushing forth from bubbling springs.

"My home is where the polar bear
Hunts for the seal and ice's glare,
And where the chubby Esquimau
With dog and sled glides o'er the snow.
By arctic winds I'm driven down
To shroud the earth in winter's gown;
I prowl around the cottage door,
And seek the chinks and Brusseled floor.

"And where the baby's snug and warm,
I steal around his little form:
And yet I have a work to do
To save the flowering bulbs for you.

I clothe the earth, and keep it warm,
And save these germs of earth from harm;
And when the sunny spring has come,
I to the widening rivers run.

"When in this humid tropic clime
I start again on the wings of time,
Ascending in the balmy air,
Until I reach a current where
The Northern trades are passing nigh,
And then again I say good-bye,
Good-bye, dear flowers of the torrid zone,
I'll go again to my native home."

A HORNET'S NEST.

The sentry stood out at the door,
  And winked and bustled around;
He sallied in and told a score
  That an enemy he had found.

I threw a stick at the hornet's nest,
  And one came buzzing by;
I started to run my very best,
  But he caught me on the eye.

I threw myself down on the ground,
  And rolled and writhed in pain:
But no relief down there I found,
  For they darted and came again.

So up I got, and away I went,
Surrounded by a swarm;
And in that race I did repent
I gave such wild alarms.

I slapped my hands and scratched about,
And did many things in vain;
I pulled the deserted stingers out,
And felt the smarting pain.

I ne'er had been in such distress,
But always will refrain
From clubbing of a hornet's nest,
Since I have felt such pain.

Now, all you boys who think it's fun
To throw your shafts and darts,
Had better prepare some place to run
Before you make such starts.

THE CUNNING, COVETOUS JEW.

"Come in, my friend, and see my stock,
My goods are nice and new;
I've everything, from hat to frock,"
Said the cunning, covetous Jew.
They're always hanging out in front
To catch and lure you in;
No matter if your speech is blunt,
They want the shining tin.

"Try on this coat, it is all wool,
    And woven nice and new."
And on the shoulder it is too full,
    But you know a cunning Jew.
"How do you like this suit of black,
    It's imported goods clear through?"
And, grasping a handful in the back,
    Cried out: "It's shust a fit for you!"

"You see it's lined with satin cloth,
    And sewed with silken thread,"
And to tell the truth 'twas eaten by moth.
    But, " 'Tis excellent!" he said.
"Now try this vest of latest style,
    It's bound all round before,"
And on the tag I see the while
    'Twas made in eighty-four.

"Eight dollars is the price of it,
    And that is very cheap.
I cannot fall a single bit."
    He at the cost mark peeped.
He feigns he's selling out at cost,
    And cannot fall, be-joses,
Without incurring heavy loss,
    He'd swear by holy Moses.

But, by the by, we pretend to go,
    And offer but dollars six.
"I cannot take that price!" said Steve,
    But we've heard of Jewish tricks.

We move along, as if to go,
  And watch that cunning Jew;
He could not take, he pretended so,
  But he'll wrap it up for you.

"Now can I sell you a hat or tie?"
  He'll show you through the stock;
You cannot go unless you buy,
  At prices at bed-rock.
He's always selling out at cost,
  And tells a woeful tale;
He's had a fire, a damage loss,
  The reason for the sale.

"Now call again," he'll say to you,
  One hand upon your shoulder—
An instinct of an artful Jew,
  To cheat and be the bolder.
He casts a wink at an elder son
  To signify he's done you.
And that's the way the thing is done
  By the cunning, covetous Hebrew.

And thus he goes from year to year,
  A-selling out so cheap;
And yet he has a conscience clear,
  And money by the heap.
Though all was made by selling out
  Away below the cost.
And that's the way this Jew came out
  Who sold and always lost.

THE RAGGEDY GAL.

The raggedy gal is nurse for ma,
 And chores about the house:
She makes the children cake and slaw,
 And good old apple sauce.
Her flaky pudding is so fine
 And colored nice and brown,
And served with milk from fattest kine.
 And sugar from the town.
 Oh! the raggedy gal, the raggedy gal,
 Encircled with a balmoral!

She gave us peaches from the trees,
 And peanuts from the ground,
Some pretty shells from out the sea,
 And played like she was clown.
Then up and down the road we went,
 A-drawing of a cart,
And from the dusty path we sent
 The grasshopper quick and sharp.
 Oh! the raggedy gal, the raggedy gal,
 Encircled with a balmoral!

The raggedy gal will care for baby,
 Playing in the pleasant shade,
Just as happy as a May bee
 Out in gaudy dress parade.

Little songs she's always humming,
　All must bow and nod and sing;
Little feet are nimbly shuffling
　　To the trumpet's twangling ring.
　　　Oh! the raggedy gal, the raggedy gal,
　　　Encircled with a balmoral!

We love the chubby ragged lady
　For the sweet meats and the buns;
No matter if her dress is fady,
　　She has friends, and loving ones.
Children play about her jolly,
　And press her gently at the knees;
They enjoy such pranks and folly—
　　Pleasures for their childish ease.
　　　Oh! the raggedy gal, the raggedy gal,
　　　Encircled with a balmoral!

She is queen out making sunshine,
　Gathering moss from off the logs,
Swinging in the corded grape vines,
　　And seeking the curious of the bogs
She is captain of the party
　As the maranders scour the woods;
They are laughing loud and hearty,
　　Gathering berries ripe and good.
　　　Oh! the raggedy gal, the raggedy gal,
　　　Encircled with a balmoral!

Oh! the sweetest thing is the raggedy gal,
Singing songs of fal-de-ral.
She has access to the cellar,
Giving out the apples mellow;
She has all the pantry care—
Pies and cakes so rich and rare:
She must give the urchins some.
Bless the children! this is fun.
    Oh! the good old raggedy, raggedy gal,
    Encircled with a balmoral!

THE WELLS TRAGEDY.

THE FOUR INNOCENTS.

As four small boys were at work one day
   Picking strawberries so beautiful and red,
Their hearts were very blithe and gay,
   And the sun shone bright o'erhead.

Work to them was naught but play,
   They did it with a will;
Adroitly they worked away
   Their vessels for to fill.

The father came the work to inspect.
   But ne'er tried to assist:
His mind was crazed and did reflect
   In the ways of a pessimist.

Their childish glee told the work was done,
    As the playful little boys
Were starting homeward so full of fun,
    With such cheerful, childish joys.

The father lured them on the way
    By scenes at a wayside well,
Where a woodchuck burrowed in the clay,
    Which served as their parting knell.

While looking in the quaint old well,
    The father pushed them in.
Oh! such a sight!   Oh! who can tell
    Of such a crime and sin!

They dropped beneath the turbid wave,
    They climbed the rugged wall,
And looking at their father, crazed,
    They pitifully did call.

"Oh! father, save!   What have we done
    That you desire to kill?
Our task we've never tried to shun:
    Oh! spare us, please grant our will!"

But on he went with furious rage,
    And crushed one's little head:
The father had them in a cage—
    Their wounds profusely bled.

They caught the parent by the leg
  And writhed as he pushed them under,
And for their lives they begged and plead—
  Their bodies he rent asunder.

The mother saw from a distant place
  Something she could not descry.
And, speeding onward with quickened pace,
  She heard the children cry.

O God! the sight that met her eyes,
  As she peered down in the deep.
She heard such pitiful, pleading cries,
  But two had gone to sleep.

She wrung her hands and cried aloud,
  And prayed God her children to save:
Behold! there came a rescue crowd,
  And snatched two from the grave.

The mother released two only sons
  Out of a madman's grasp—
A mother's love is the only one
  That will forever last.

But the rent that's in that mother's heart
  No time can ever heal,
The jar that set their lives apart:
  The scenes about the well.

Her darlings lay upon the ground,
　Their spirits gone to heaven;
No trace of life in them was found
　Save the promise God has given.

No place can shut the soul within—
　It rests outside the tomb;
The one that dies and is free from sin
　Finds in God's temple a boon.

MAXWELL.

In early days, when wild woods was rife,
The people sought to better their life;
To join their mites was a common rule,
And build a rural district school.
So the people here did just the same,
And built a cabin before the frame;
And many a tale the by-gones tell
Of how we courted sweet Rosie Nell.

The older boys would cut the wood,
And do such things as they thought they should.
While the girls would sweep the rustic floor,
And hang around the open door.
We jumped the rope and dropped the 'kerchiefs too,
And passed the dreary winters through;
We stood in a line our lessons to spell.
And sought a place by sweet Rosie Nell.

A hole in the wall transmitted light,
And the old rude benches were a sight;
You'd see them setting along the wall,
For ne'er a one had a back at all.
We'd sit there like a crouching 'coon,
And throw some wads across the room—
For this is what the old folks tell
Of the pranks they played with sweet Rosie Nell.

MAXWELL.

Some gads were cut, and hid around,
For those who played and acted the clown;
And often it happened the culprit missed,
And an innocent back would writhe and twist

Beneath the flail of the teaching one,
To pay the debt of the laugh and fun.
For this is the way they cut a swell,
And attracted the attention of sweet Rosie Nell.

The windows sometimes were paper gauze;
We had a code of well-written laws:
The absconder must always meet the brunt
For taking a truant rabbit hunt;
The teacher would often make the plan,
And often he had but one eye or hand,
And yet he would act the dude and swell
To gain the confidence of sweet Rosie Nell.

And this is the way old Maxwell grew,
Until the district was cut in two.
One part was east and one was west—
'Tis hard to tell you which was best;
For often we met of evenings to see
Which was the best at a spelling bee,
And much was the cunning that was used and well
To be best man with sweet Rosie Nell.

But then there came some better days,
The boys rode out in one-horse chaise,
And now our name is spread afar
Since we've passed the code of the three R's.
We are keeping abreast and with the times
By making of teachers and divines;
And now we return from a distance to tell
Of how we courted sweet Rosie Nell.

9

THE KISSING BUG.

Some ladies are afraid of a kissing bug,
    And cannot sleep o' night.
And yet they embrace and kiss a thug
    And think it out of sight.

This bug appears when snug in bed,
    And you are sound asleep:
You'll feel it crawling o'er your head,
    And touch your rosy cheeks.

He steals a kiss, then off he goes,
    The subject sleeping sound:
He leaves the impression of his nose—
    In the morning it is found.

You'll know this bug, with tweezers sharp,
    And beak that's very black;
You'll feel so queer about the heart
    As he takes a dainty smack.

This is a freak, as we have found,
    While walking in the park:
That ladies pass their kisses 'round
    When it is growing dark.

This bug has plenty of cologne,
    And smells like foaming beer:
He feels himself so much at home
    When on a lady's ear.

Now, ladies, you should guard your mouth,
　As you have had some tips,
Or this vagrant will break in your house
　And kiss your rosy lips..

THE HAPPY FARMER.

Did you ever see a farmer, by jo,
Out in his little potato patch to hoe,
With the weeds falling dead all around
On the dark, fertile, gopherized ground?
It is quite a pretty sight to see,
With the Colorado beetle on his knee;
But he is a happy farmer, just so.

Did you ever see a farmer, by jo,
Out in his little meadow to mow,
And the children all coming out to play,
Always getting in the sturdy farmer's way?
It is a sight quite pretty, I would say,
And his good wife is tedding of the hay;
But he is a happy farmer, just so.

Did you ever see a farmer, by jo,
As he goes out his seed to sow,
With the midges in his wheat,
And the cheat blossoms sweet
As he plods across the field?
He knows there'll be no yield;
But he is a happy farmer, just so.

Did you ever see a farmer, by jo,
As his prospects are brightening up so,
With the pumpkin on the vine,
And his hogs, and his kine?
But the cholera will come,
And the fatal black tongue—
But he is a happy farmer, just so.

Did you ever see a farmer, by jo,
As he hitches up his team to go
And gather the golden grain,
In the snow and the rain
And bring it to the barn?
Which is the custom on the farm—
But he is a happy farmer, just so.

Did you ever see a farmer, by jo,
With his produce all heaped in a row,
As he starts for the town
And the prices have come down?
Then he trudges all around,
And no market is found;
But he is a happy farmer, just so.

Did you ever see a farmer, by jo,
Under mortgages and debts to grow?
As he starts to go away
Some dude will halloo "Hey!"
Then the farmer will look around,
And the imp can't be found,
For he is a muscled farmer, just so.

Did you ever see a farmer, by jo,
As the Master is calling him to go
Unto his final rest
With the good and oppressed?
For he was a son of toil
In this world of turmoil—
But he was a happy farmer, by jo.

JOHN CHINAMAN, MY JOE.

Of all the men I chance to meet,
In crowded lane or on the street,
With blouse around his chubby beak,
And wooden shoes upon his feet,
    Is John Chinaman, my Joe John,
    John Chinaman, my Joe.

When in a crowd he'll hustle through,
He wore a plaid he called a "queue,"
You'll know him by the antique shoe,
And eyes that's just set in askew.
    John Chinaman, my Joe John,
    John Chinaman, my Joe.

He wore a cap drawn o'er his skull,
And mice and rats they filled his hull,
His chop-sticks came unto a lull
As he smoked his pipe of opiates full,
    John Chinaman, my Joe John,
    John Chinaman, my Joe.

A mandarin, we call the chap
In wooden shoes and turban cap,
And beneath his chest he wore a flap,*
This mulligan man with braided plat,
    John Chinaman, my Joe John,
    John Chinaman, my Joe.

You'll find him in a laundry shop
Filled with relics unto the top:
A little rice to fill his chops,
And a couch within on which he lops,
    John Chinaman, my Joe John,
    John Chinaman, my Joe.

He little eats, and little drinks,
And of his soul he little thinks;
His almond eyes he blinks and blinks,
His pig-tail queue he plaits and kinks.
    John Chinaman, my Joe John,
    John Chinaman, my Joe.

His complexion is of a tawny hue,
And stature like a Chinese shrew.
His manners he cannot renew,
Except by the teaching of Confuciu.
    John Chinaman, my Joe John,
    John Chinaman, my Joe.

* Flap is used for the word apron.

Some day he'll pass through deathly throes,
And go where all good Chinamen goes,
And where that is we do not know.
It may be heaven, or it may be—so.
        John Chinaman, my Joe John,
        John Chinaman, my Joe.

And here we'll leave the mulligan man,
And all akin to the Orient clan;
There's vice enough in the heathen land
To bring that kingdom to a strand.
        John Chinaman, my Joe John,
        John Chinaman, my Joe.

THE PAINTER POET, J. W. RILEY.

'Twas on a painter's scaffold,
    Adorning the faded walls,
That our poet obtained his lessons
    In those scenes aglow for all.

But he's nobler than a painter,
    With an eye for beauteous scroll,
And has penned such words of wisdom
    As his thoughts in music roll.

'Tis a gift of art so cunning
    To write in words of sweetest rhythm,
And thus portray the scenes of nature,
    Or the seraphs God has given.

But the poet pictures nicely
  Beautiful things out on the lea,
As he sketches through his optics
  Greenest swards in waves like sea.

With now and then a fragrant flower,
  Whose sweet aroma fills the breeze,
Encircled with such ruddy petals
  The heart's delight in quest of ease.

The pen is talking of the image
  In the mind or of the soul,
As it speeds by inspiration
  To attain the good or goal.

Thus we find the Hoosier Poet,
  In thoughts akin to the mouldering past,
Holding forth a vivid picture
  Mirrored by the mind's reflecting cast.

More excellent writings have ne'er been given
  In a strain so rich and pure,
Flowing gently with a ripple,
  Everlasting to endure.

POCAHONTAS.

Born in the sylvan wild,
  Inured to toil and strife,
Meek and modest was the child
  Who strove a nomad life.

Amidst those of a rubicund hue,
  Painted in warlike array,
This innocent in amity grew,
  With the villagers in frolicsome play.

Daughter of the great Powhattan Chief,
  Heir to the throne of her race,
Friend to the Pilgrims in relief,
  With venison to relieve their wan grimace.

In trials and trouble she's true,
  For grandeur she surely was born;
For as soon as the war dance was through
  She brought a sweet morsel of corn.

But a noise from the rattle breaks in,
  An omen of war and of peace;
'Tis a sight in such noise and din
  To see the foe crouch for relief.

Adroitly the old chief raised
  His war club o'er his crested head,
But Providence by Pocahontas saved
  Captain Smith from the throes of the dead.

O child inspired with such love,
  Whose motives were friendly and good—
An image so pure like the dove
  Which abode on the Savior in the wood.

Now with vain design these warriors adorn,
  Sad heart, knowing secrets of right;
A message to the village is borne
  As she steals through the darkness of night.

They were saved by the warning of one,
  A goddess in savage dress,
A life like a ray of the Son
  Which God has pardoned and blessed.

She was held as a ransom of peace
  Till the red warriors mellowed in strife,
But never was her heart quite released,
  For Rodolph had made her his wife.

She was taken to the court of St. James,
  An honored and competent guest,
A wonder to those of the Thames,
  Delighted and fondly caressed.

A union of hearts and of hands,
A union of tribes and of lands,
A union of posterity still
Remains in the Old Dominion, and will

HANS SPADGENS' HEN.

Now come, old Speck, I'll make dot nest,
  And put vone dozzen in it:
You'll git some rest and I'll be bleshed
  Wid thirteen checks within it.

Just git right on these eggs ov your'n,
  And varm dee dormant germ:
I'll give dee food to hatch dee brood
  And keep dem fertile and varm.

Madam Spadgens is vanting some fowels
  To sell and buy some yarns,
And because she's none she sometimes growls
  And makes some great alarms.

Now yer set thri weeks: I'll try dem eggs
  And see der good a tall:
I'll hold dee light so nice and bright,
  And votch dee silihouette on der wall.

Oh, vife, come hor and votch right thar,
  And see if yer can skiver
If dee shadow thar is downy far,
  Or shades ov a torpid liver.

Oh, yaw, yaw, yaw! it moves! it moves!
  These eggs vill soon be checkens:
Tey'll scratch me flowers aft rainy showers,
  And then thar'll be dee dickens.

And now I has dem all but vone,
  Dee shell seems not a pippen;
I'll press it vittle gist for vun.
  Pooh! pooh! it crashed! it's rotten!

And now I has de hull of dem,
    Dee ole bird's alers clucken:
I'll build a pin to put dem in,
    To save dee flowers from thar plucken.

Now I see thass logger beers
    For me and Dolly Spadgens:
Vee'll eat sauer krout and sip about
    From dee foaming, frothy flagons.

Some fruits vee'll raise along wid checks,
    To kape from constipation:
Some grapes and eggs and yellow legs
    Will form our daily rations.

THE ROBIN.

The robin built her clever nest
    In the fork of an apple tree;
'Twas there I saw her pale red breast,
    And eggs so blue to see.

She sang a song from a tilting limb,
    'Twas early in the morn:
Her nest was filled unto the brim
    With birdies newly born.

I waved my hand above the nest,
    They chirped, and chirped again,
And stretched their necks their very best—
    'Twas only but a sham.

THE ROBIN.

The tune she sang was loud and sweet,
It soothed the young ones' breasts;
She soared away for some food to eat,
As nature had taught her best.

The young birds looked at the mother above,
  And wondered why such cheer:
'Twas the sweetest melody of family love
  That one could ever hear.

She watched the nestlings clothed in down,
  As day by day they grew,
Until their pinions feathered round,
  Then from their nest they flew.

They now are singing a robin's lay,
  As children ought to do:
It banishes sorrow from each day,
  As life they journey through.

OUR FLAG.

Our flag still waves o'er No. 9,
  It floats out from the steeple:
This is a country great and grand,
  A patriotic people.

Some heartless wretch removed it once—
  An insult to the teacher:
She played the part of Judy Punch,
  The handsome little creature.

She then procured a big pop-gun—
  It bore an ivory handle;
It reminds one of a petty tale—
  'Twill always raise a scandal.

And now the parties have taken it up.
  The hoot owl loudly screeches;
Politicians are full of sup—
  They have it in their breeches.

Patriotism is not so free
  Expressed by public speakers;
'Tis only a little bragado-hee—
  They are but office-seekers.

Just like the fox said to the ass:
  "Your ears they will betray thee,"
No matter if you have the brass
  And are working for the party.

We'll kill the goat and whip the kid
  That removed the flying missile;
Then the lady can lay down
  Her Yankee belt and pistol.

Joan of Arc was a heroine—
  She rode a flying charger:
But all there is of that teacher now:
  Her name is a little larger.

A VIEW OF NATURE.

Ambition leads to great success:
A tiresome hand is ever blessed
With all this earth doth hold
In fee or treasures of shining gold.

A shiftless person is all a glow,
Preparing a field some seeds to sow,
It may be great, it may be small,
But knowledge gained surpasses all.

A childish mind is but a blank,
Revolving around just like a crank,
Adhering to either good or bad,
Making a man out of a lad.

Proper schooling is what one needs,
Tearing away the noxious weeds.
And using skillfully a pruning knife
To shape the tree for after life.

Education is a nursery bed
Out of which our thoughts are fed,
And, judging by the streams that flow,
People may our culture know.

Good nature smiled upon the child,
Embracing him when very wild,
Inviting him to come and rest,
Peering through her folds of dress.

KIND DEEDS.

Little deeds of kindness
    Always are at hand,
Ready to remind us
    Greatness is a man.

Storing up a treasure
   Unto the garner's fill,
With a social wisdom,
   Should be our only will.

Working in the sunshine,
   With exalted cheer,
Elevating mankind,
   With nothing for to fear.

Uniting all in friendship
   Which should ever be,
Forming of a union
   To calm a troubled sea.

*   *   *   *   *

Come, board the ship that leads to life,
   Whose sails are made of love.
And banish things which lead to strife,
   And sail to God above.

THE MONON WRECK.

OUR LAST RIDE.

The train is coming yonder, near,
The conductor calls the station clear,
Then outward move the busy throng
Ready for their stepping on.

A signal waved says all is well,
And now we hear the parting bell;
The engineer opes the steam chest throes,
Then swifter than a dart she goes.

She glides along quite at her ease,
The swiftness causes a gentle breeze:
The wheels are creaking on the frosty rails.
Just like a bird she nimbly sails.

One mile is passed and all is fun:
Two miles are made—the thing is done:
We are crossing over Sugar creek bridge,
And starting on the graded ridge.

She strikes against a broken rail,
When all the cars it does derail,
And down they plunge into the deep,
A depth of more than sixty feet.

She rolled over just afore and aft,
The occupants turning like a shaft,
Before she reaches this mournful place,
Where each the other's soul embraced.

A silence fell upon the crew,
As if they knew not what to do;
Then came sad and lamenting cries
From a wreck of cars as fine as flies,

Tears are flowing thick and fast
From every one of the mangled mass;
And, laying there, we hear their prayers,
Asking the Lord to relieve their cares:

"Our Heavenly Father! wilt Thou draw near,
And hear our woe in supplication here;
Save us from this wreck of flame,
Where dearest comrades have been slain."

To the nearest town a messenger made,
While on the ground the dead are laid.
Oh, how terrible are the moaning sighs,
With pitiful appeals and last good-byes!

But there they lay on the crimson snow —
Their hearts have ceased to ebb and flow;
Quite as cold as a frozen chunk,
With a lady's heart upon a stump.

Which was so far from her native home:
The ancient city of old Rome:
Never again to reach that clime,
And hear the bell of St. Peter's chime.

And now the flames begin to light
The demolished cars, which adds to fright,
For fear that all will burn to death,
Oh, God! intervene and save the rest!

And yonder in the wreck I see
A man that's pinioned down by the knee,
And hear him calmly for to say:
"Cut, oh, cut my leg away!"

But a jack-crew from the mail caboose
Is now applied and lets him loose,
With many thanks to these brave men—
For greater heroes ne'er have been.

There was a mother, frantic and wild,
Looking for her little child,
Which in her fright had run away
To the nearest house of that sad fray.

And as that mother paced to and fro,
She found some footprints in the snow.
And, leaping onward with breathless bound,
Her loving daughter soon was found.

And such a meeting ne'er has been—
It moistened the eyes of the bravest men,
While in her arms she clasped so dear
The object of her joy and fear.

But four are dead—they speak no more:
The Savior has their souls in store,
Awaiting of the Judgment Day,
Where all is good, or sad dismay.

A REVIVAL MEETING.

'Tis long to be remembered,
Those grand old meetings of yore,
Those songs of cheer which soothed the ear—
'Twas never so before.
None tired by oft times meeting,
Nor love of brotherly greeting;
'Twas a Christians' old reunion,
Partaking of the Lord's communion.

To preach the gospel was God's command,
Preach it boldly in every land,
Teach it plainly in every truth,
Gleaning carefully, like ancient Ruth;
Converting sinners to God's embrace,
To bear the cross with heavenly grace,
And be a soldier in the glorious strife,
And make atonement for a future life.

Be Christ's disciples, and fear no ill,
And fearlessly teach the Savior's will;
And make it plain to every man,
Proving all things from a Bible stand.
The work must be so good and true
To insure the soul its passport through
To the holy city not made with hands,
Where sits the king of hosanna bands.

The streets are paved in purest gold.
And altars adorned in emeralds old.
And with sapphires and rubies just awry,
Which shines like constellations in the sky.
No crown of thorns upon the head,
But one of joy and love instead.
And thus remains the Christian fraternity
Throughout the ages of all eternity.

A myriad of voices with anthem ring.
While noble evangelists lead the van:
Like David's harp, it cheers the soul,
And encourages one to attain the goal
Which rests beyond the starry sky,
Where never a soul will say good-bye,
But rest eternal around the throne,
And join with the saints in "Home, Sweet Home."

MY MARY OF MISSOURI.

My Mary of Missouri
    Was quick, and blithe, and shy,
A goddess of simplicity,
    With dark and hazel eye.
She was as modest as could be,
    And playful as a kitten:
I watched the expression of her face
    To see she meant no mitten.

I advanced a little farther
　And mildly said: "Kind lady,
Let's seat ourselves down by the brook,
　And converse where it is shady."
Her cheeks were reddened to a blush,
　But cutely she assented;
We talked about the pinks and ferns,
　And things so complimented.

Her nature was a child of mirth,
　As things of nature blended;
I spoke in tones quite soft and low,
　In words of love intended.
The query, though, I never put,
　But matched some buds and cherries,
And watched the mirror of a soul—
　'Twas like two image fairies.

I concealed my thoughts from one I loved,
　With flowing, shining tresses;
Her face was fair, I do declare,
　And lips were pure caresses.
The day was calm and very warm,
　The woods were fairly humming,
When two young hearts were beating fast—
　Like pheasants they were drumming.

We started off a-rambling
　Among the dells and bowers;
We culled the sweetest roses,
　And all the pretty flowers.

The cows lowed in the pastures.
  And birds were singing sweet;
My eyes were on those dimples,
  Like rubies, in her cheeks.

I moved to her some closer,
  And looked gently in her face
And threw my arms around
  Her neat and slender waist.
My heart felt like 'twas yearning
  As neared the time to part—
Just then I did discover
  She had my soul and heart.

I asked a future meeting.
  She bowed with graceful bliss,
And, improving precious moments,
  I stole a pleasant kiss.
I vowed that I would have her,
  If ever such could be,
That she should be my darling
  And I her fiance.

I asked her out for walking—
  'Twas only for a plea,
And quickly she responded:
  "I'll journey long with thee."
Then raising her golden bracelet—
  The fairest in the land—
I placed the shining signet
  Of love upon her hand.

'Twas settled then, forever,
   That we would never part:
That I would have a better half,
   And she a loving heart.
A cottage on the hill revealed
   A pleasant country home,
Where I reigned jointly as a king,
   And she heir to the throne.

MONEY MOVES.

Men's hearts are moved by money,
   As the wind moves the snow;
And it is a great incentive
   For them to make a show.

From the peasant in his cottage
   To the king upon the throne,
You'll find the power of money
   To be the whole backbone.

The jingling of the guinea,
   And the shining of the dust,
Will wear away corrosion
   And brighten up the rust.

It will bring us to our duty
   When everything else would fail;
It will stay us in our business,
   If our efforts are but stale.

MARY'S LAMB.

Mary's lamb is dead long ago,
  But young ones just as gay
Are running in the fields, you know,
  And just as nice at play.

MARY'S LAMB.

The road that Mary went to school
  Is now macadam or a pike;
The boys and girls all break the rules
  By riding on a bike.

The old school house is torn away,
　　No trace of it is found:
But a new one built in modern ways
　　Now stands upon the ground.

The lamb that ate from Mary's hand
　　Has greater advantages now:
Since Grace a new invention planned,
　　It sucks the Jersey cow.

The Jersey loved the lambkin so
　　She treated it with pride,
And everywhere that she would go,
　　It trotted by her side.

The children say they will not release
　　The lamb from off the farm.
And that they want its pretty fleece
　　To make their stocking yarn.

And as the years are passing by,
　　You need not think it strange
If airships sail beneath the sky,
　　Like meteors in their range.

LANGUAGE.

Language flows from the lips of him
　　Who speaks with cultured tongue:
It's music just as choice as when
　　The organ's keys are sprung.

But children learn without a will
  Those sweetest rippling notes,
Absorbing of the teacher's skill—
  His actions largely floats.

Good manners should predominate:
  Use diligence in every plan:
With care in showing to create,
  Will make the better man.

THE WARSHIP MAINE.

The Maine moved onward in her glory,
  To the tropic isle of Spain,
Where she anchored in the harbor,
  And freedom shrieked in vain.
She floated o'er the foaming waters,
  Like the soaring albatross,
When the roaring billows threatened
  And the sea was upward tossed.

Then she sailed into Havana harbor,
  With her ensign to the breeze—
Just a thing of perfect beauty,
  Valiant sailors at their ease.
But the fiendish Spanish warriors,
  Filled with murder and rapine,
Fired a shot from just beneath her,
  From an electric magazine.

The good old ship was rent asunder,
    And our heroes writhed with pain;
And now this nation throbs with fervor
    To redress the wrongs to the battle Maine.
This brings to bear the Monroe Doctrine,
    Severing chains of bonded men,
Dating back to some old country
    By colonizing and ties of ken.

Uncle Sam will soon be heeded
    By ancient powers of kings and queens,
Which lie along the old world oceans,
    Great in pomp and showy scenes.
Every patriotic American citizen
    Scorns intrusion by a foe,
Fearless, dauntless, waiting patient
    For their orders for to go

And uphold the Starry Banner
    Of the Union strong and grand,
Sailing outward on the ocean
    To the shores of another land.
We don't desire the Isle of Cuba,
    But are longing for to see
Her name inscribed like other nations
    With a banner pure and free.

THANKSGIVING.

The turkeys are so fat and nice,
　　And bounteous crops are clear;
We give our thanks for the nation's life,
　　With a festival once a year.

In the days of sixty-three and four,
　　When no one knew her fate,
We put our trust in Almighty Power
　　To save the old Ship of State.

And in the end the right prevailed,
　　No ribs or keel were rent.
But onward against the tide she sailed,
　　On a glorious mission bent.

And when the close was surely known,
　　Our hearts beat free but still;
The cause of liberty was widely sown
　　O'er woodland, vale and hill.

No color line divides us now.
　　Our wounds have healed quite well;
And all to the same Omnipotent bow,
　　With free, unrestrained good will.

We thank the Lord who gave the strength
　　This blessing to secure,
And bring a struggle to an end
　　We hope will long endure.

No men are now dragged through the street.
And papers burned with ire;
The press is free with moral sheet,
If it can find a buyer.

No railroads on the tunnel plan,
But on an elevation,
And he who rides must be a man—
A part of a living nation.

Now all of this was brought about
By pluck and might together:
The boys in blue did freely shout—
Their blood did stain the heather.

And thus we have Thanksgiving Day
To commune and bless each other,
When we can sing and talk and pray,
And commingle like a brother.

A COUNTRY SAWMILL WAGON.

Some wheels were thick and some were thin.
I blocked the log on with a pin.
And through the hounds was thrust a pole
To stop the haggard-looking hole.

Some chains were large and some were small,
And some could not be found at all;
It is the very best pattern of the kind.
And neither wheel will fall in line.

A wonderful thing is the coupling pin—
It's crooked without and crooked within;
The bolsters were staid up with a wire,
Which played a tune like an ancient lyre.

And in the world it has no peer—
It's rattled along for many a year;
But I must confide unto a friend:
It's good enough to keep and lend.

It has gone through woods and through the mire,
And over the rocks which sparkled fire;
But on it went, with teamster friend,
Until it met a final end.

It struck a bowlder a heavy jolt,
Which broke the axles and severed a bolt;
Then came a crash amidst mud and rain—
There in a heap it still remains.

A CHARACTERIZED SCHOOL.

In the upper camp the boss is large,
He runs his boat just like a barge,
And now I think he is aground—
You ought to hear him blow and sound.

This teacher's name is Georgie Shultz,
He courts the girls by feeling pulse;
And when he's far in the abyss,
He seals the bargain with a kiss.

In the lower camp the bees are thick,
And Homer stirs 'em with a stick;
He bids them all to be quite still,
His voice is very harsh and shrill—
You'd think it was a raging storm,
Or the devil's imp in uniform.

A COUNTRY ELDER.

An elder once, whose name was Claron,
   Was hunting cows one starry night;
He did not meet the rose of Sharon,
   But fell into a pretty plight.

By chance he passed a suitor's mansion,
   And leaned so gently on the gate:
As two young men went by to sanction,
   This praying elder pulled his freight.

He turned his face in shadowed darkness,
   For fear he would suspicion 'rouse:
"Halloo, my boy, bad time o' night
   That you are out a-hunting cows."

13

"This is a sight quite pretty, deacon,
    Silent prayers are heard above;
No wonder that you look so sneakin'
    When you're out a-making love

"With another man's poor maiden,
    When he's off a-teaching school;
Just because he's heavy laden,
    You try to play him for a fool."

DEATH OF D. W. VOORHEES.

He has served at the bar of justice,
    With all his skill and power;
His strength was that of a giant,
    An orator was his dower.

His voice was sweet and musical,
    The ear 'twould fairly charm;
His metaphors like the Savior's,
    This hero of the farm.

He's served in the nation's Congress,
    And did his work so well
That all are singing praises
    Who mourn his loss to tell.

He served the people valiantly,
    Their cause he did defend;
Like Cincinnatus, the chieftain,
    He served them to the end.

Oh, the noble things of wisdom
   For which he gave his might,
And stood so peer and manly
   Until he got it right.

He advocated building
   A national library tall and wide,
And lived to see it completed,
   Whatever may betide.

But the Savior's knocking, calling
   For spirits when they're right,
And taking home his children
   From darkness into light.

So He claimed this national hero,
   Whose name was rightly given,
To come and meet the angels
   Before the bar of heaven.

And in the hour of darkness,
   When the stars were shining bright,
The soul of the Indianian
   Took its upward course or flight.

THE FROG.

The frog sits on the old mill dam,
   And catches bugs and flies,
And when he hears a noise at hand,
   He just leaps in and dives.

You can see his kicking legs,
    At which you're sure to gaze,
And see the moving of the dregs
    In little circling waves.

THE FROG.

And when he reaches the other shore,
    You'll hear him halloo again;
It may be like some distant roar,
    Or like the bleating lamb.

And as you're passing some old pond,
    You'd think the demon's there,
To hear them halloo from each frond,
    A legion of voices rare.

And when you look around to find
    What made the tragic sound,
You'll see that you are far behind—
    No trace of them is found.

And if you chance to locate one,
    You need not be surprised,
For just above the slimy scum
    You'll see his piercing eyes.

And if the coast is not so clear
    That he would like to land,
He'll duck again, so much in fear,
    And seek some other strand.

The tree-frog is so very odd,
    And yet he's very strange:
His color changes from a clod
    To things on which they range.

PEARL BRYAN'S FATE.

Pretty Pearl Bryan had an elegant home,
With flowers and green pastures whither she roamed;
Her face like a rosebud, and teeth snowy white,
A gem of pure beauty—a star of the night.

There came to this cottage, in care of Will Wood,
A wooer, Scott Jackson, an imp of the lewd,
And betrayed this kind maiden, her heart he did break,
Who laid down her life for a villain's sake.

He absconded to Cincinnati, and dentistry took.
And left a true love he willfully forsook,
To pine in true nature—a false, fickle friend,
He never intended his ways for to mend.

There came a quick message: "Oh! come to me, dear,
I never once thought how I treated you here.
Oh, come to me, darling.   I'll make it all right:
Make your departure in shadow of night."

Shrill shrieked the whistle, she then bade adieus,
And soon there was flying this wonderful news.
She's safe in Queen City, a medium is found,
And her future destiny this witch does expound.

She goes to the station her steps to retake,
Where Walling consoles her, which is a mistake.
A carriage is procured for making a drive,
When this poor girl is last seen alive.

A darkey was secured as coachman in disguise,
To the shore of Kentucky they quickly arrive;
These steeds of assassins are making good stride
To a place in the bushes, their mischief to hide.

The carriage is stopped by the side of the road,
Where two cruel wretches have landed their load;
With cocaine and dagger these fiends, 'tis said,
Relieved this poor damsel of a beautiful head.

When the moon's rays reflected the bright, shining
    steel,
She fainted within and began for to kneel.
"Oh, God, save the distressed, and care for me quick!
Take me to heaven." Then came the death lick.

She sank on the leaflets, her blood stained the thyme;
Thus ended the most brutish of modern crime—
All for the lusts or passions of men,
Whose doom is the scaffold or work in the pen.

The darkey is frightened nigh unto death,
And flees with the horses that's throbbing for breath,
And leaves the two murderers afoot for to flee,
With the head in a satchel, as bloody as can be.

A search of their clothing reveals spots crimson red,
But where, Oh! where is the poor victim's head?
'Tis sunk in the river, or hid in the ground,
Never, 'tis supposed, by man to be found.

Now these Herods are landed inside of a jail,
And leave the old parents to weep and to wail
The loss of their darling, so dear unto them,
Slain by assassins—imps of good men.

A mob is now raising: they quake, it is said,
And feel the cold chills at the loss of their heads.
An appeal is now taken to Kentucky for fear
'Tis only a-hastening to meet the cold bier.

These men they must hang, the jury did say,
Until they are dead, a debt for to pay,
For killing a maiden just in her beauty and bloom,
And now lies headless in a mouldering tomb.

They ascended the scaffold—a ransom of blood;
The trap door is sprung, and Oh! what a thud!
Two bodies are swinging at the end of a cord,
Their spirits ascended to the court of our Lord.

No telling which way the spirits will go—
Whether 'tis up, or far, far below;
One thing is certain: 'tis better by odds
To be a good person, a child of God's.

BOTANICAL SCIENCE.

Our botany comes from Linnæus of old,
And to my mind it seems so cold;
Peering through those stalks and stipes,
My mind does wander as I write.

By subterranean we view beneath the ground,
And find those things that support the frond,
And merge them into parts that suit
All other ones above the root.

By aerial we view the crown,
Within which the germ is found,
As it nods in the waving air,
Closed within its capsule hair.

And as the petals die and go,
The seed is ready for to sow,
Which is done by nature's hand,
Seeding all the flowery land.

By the biting of the frost
The strength of nature all is lost;
The shell is cracked, the stoma opes,
And in the air the seed now floats.

THE CRITIC PRO TEM.

A critic once had lots of cheek,
He treated people very indiscreet;
To slander them he thought it fun—
The imp, the rascal thus begun.

He sought the weak to get a clew,
His very language would make one spew,
And would throw the bile from off the liver—
The rubbish of this grammar-giver.

By chance he thought he'd change the scene
And introduce a weather bulletin;
But by the by it proved so hard—
The signal came on a mourning card.

It seemed to him to be most neat
To brand the pupils of things not meek;
But all of this is like one vain
Seeking others to lay the blame.

WABASH COLLEGE.

In days of forests primeval,
   When people knew little but roam,
There arose an enlightening upheaval
   To educate people at home.

WABASH COLLEGE.

The idea was sown to germinate
   In an edifice great and grand,
'Twas not known 'twould terminate
   With such fame throughout the land.

Its name was christened in glory
   By those who carried it through;
Their heads grew frail and quite hoary—
   'Twas greater than anyone knew.

It grew like a thing of God's rearing,
   Slowly and firmly, by degrees,
By mites and similar clearings
   By donors like Whitlock and Simon Yandes.

There's knowledge for every poor creature
   That thirsts to illumine the soul;
'Tis this the embodied great feature
   To reach the enlightening goal.

The builders were men of great station,
   Achieving and embellishing a land,
Adorning the might of a nation
   Which forever and ever shall stand.

Already its fame's unbounded,
   By the speeches and literature of those
Who have passed the degrees of her portals
   And astonished her friends and her foes.

Come all and drink of the fountain
   Which develops soul, body and mind,
And try like Moses the mountain,
   And see what jewel you'll find.

JIM ELMORE'S BEST.

Jim Elmore, the sweet poet of Ripley township, has given us the following seasonable gem:

> In the spring of the year,
>   When the blood is too thick,
> There is nothing so rare
>   As the sassafras stick.
> It cleans up the liver,
>   it strengthens the heart,
> And to the whole system
>   New life doth impart.
>
> Sassafras, oh, sassafras!
> Thou art the stuff for me!
> And in the spring I love to sing,
>   Sweetest sassafras, of thee.

When the Journal last week received a poem extolling the virtues of sassafras, to which poem was affixed the signature of James B. Elmore, we thought that the poet was nodding. The poem failed to contain the fire and the sweet rhythmical flow which characterizes the productions of the genius of old Ripley, still it was published for the sake of the signature it bore, as, indeed, are many other productions we wot of in the leading papers and magazines of the land.

We are glad to state this week that the poem bore a forged name. Mr. Elmore didn't write it, as the following from him will show:

"Mr. Editor—There was a piece of stale poetry in your most excellent paper of last week on sassafras, which was attributed to James B. Elmore. I would say it is no child of mine. It is an illegitimate off-cast, or else its father would have owned it. My poems are printed over my signature. The following is a genuine in compliment to the so-called fake:

DUDES AND SASSAFRAS.

Some people feign would be a poet
    With their cheek of brazen brass,
As they fill their empty stomachs
    With the juice of sassafras.

They are dudes from in the city,
    With a pole and line for bass,
As they stroll by sparkling brooklets
    Hunting roots of sassafras.

Some bring their paramour and flagons
    Filled with corn fermented gas,
As they walk the dells and valleys
    In pursuit of sassafras.

When their blood is dark and ruddy,
  And their skin is a mottled mass,
They take a small decoction
  From the roots of sassafras.

Some mistake the characteristics
  Of this tree with boughs like tinted grass,
And have used the nauseous elder,
  Which removed their brains in mass.

Now when your mind is wandering,
  And your meter is stale in cast,
Don't insinuate on bards and farmers
  But just take your sassafras.

THE COUNTRY BOY.

THE country boy is born amidst the broad fields and lovely forests, and is monarch of all he surveys. He enjoys all the pleasures of the farm, and learns to work at will, which gives him health, strength and a good constitution. He looks into nature with an ever wakeful eye, which is giving culture to his mind and giving him an education greater than the dry printed matter of a dozen books. He is the idol of the household, doing errands for his mother until he is old enough to drive a horse and use a plow; then he is in the care of his father. But he never forgets the kind, gentle words of a fond, loving mother. He is in the fields every day with the men, and is being skilled in the arts of farming; and, growing up to manhood with his father's business, his keen perception take it all in at a glance. He is inured to toil, and is not afraid to work. He learns the hardships and privations which sometimes befall the farmers when the season is not favorable for a crop.

This little fellow breathes the pure, wholesome air, saturated with the odor of a thousand blossoms, and he brings the cows home from the pastures, which furnished the scene for M. H. Krout's poem, "Little Brown Hands":

"They drive home the cows from the pasture,
　Up through the long, shady lane,
Where the quail whistles loud in the wheat fields
　That are yellow with ripening grain.
They toss the new hay in the meadow,
　They gather the elder-blooms white.
They find where the dusky grapes purple
　In the soft-tinted October light.
They know where the apples hang ripest
　And are sweeter than Italy's wines.
They know where the fruit hangs the thickest
　On the long, thorny blackberry vines."

In the summer time these boys go barefooted, and sometimes poorly clothed; and they chase the brilliant-hued butterfly in his flight from flower to flower, and are so alert as to bring him down with a single swoop of their hats. It is a great pleasure to them to ramble in the woods on days when not at work, and see the pretty birds and playful squirrel leap from bough to bough. They gather the sweetest flowers for bouquets, and berries for to eat. They go a-fishing down to the little brook that runs through the pasture, and catch the red-sided minnows, of which they are as proud as if they had found a gold coin. How proud they are when they can use their father's gun and go hunting all by themselves! It may be

that when they find game they will be so anxious that
they will forget to put down powder, and have to return home without any fun; but they have to learn,
and will know better next time. You must not forget
that these boys are only small men, upon whose shoul-
ders the great ship of state rests for her future existence; and they must not be kept too close at home.
They must be allowed to go to town and see the cars
and shows, and all the amusements possible, for it
leaves impressions on their minds which the cares of
a lifetime cannot obliterate. These things make up
the garner of the mind, and furnish it so bountifully
with food, which portray these beautiful lines:

"Then Nature, the old nurse, took the boy upon her
        knee,
    Saying: 'Here is a story book thy father has given
        to thee.'"

They must have some schooling, so they can apply
themselves better to their task, and when they get an
opportunity to go to school, I assure you that they
will improve the time. They seem to apply themselves better to their books than the city youth, who
have a great deal better opportunities, as they have so
little to do, and have so much longer terms of school.
But they should bear in mind that there is no gain
without great effort on their part, and that prosperity
is not a child of sloth. It may be that they neglect

12

their studies for the pleasures of the city, which are very enticing to the young and demoralizing in effect.

Abraham Lincoln, who was nicknamed "The Rail-Splitter," was a country boy, and learned to read by the light of a tallow candle while his mother spun stocking yarn with her humming wheel. James A. Garfield was another, who drove a horse on the tow-path for a canal boat. And William Henry Harrison was another, who was dubbed the log cabin candidate. But still they arose to fame, and serve as a useful example to many a boy to encourage him in his efforts. But these are only a few of the many instances I might cite to you where farmers' boys have arisen to fame. No wonder that Robert Burns wrote: "Many a noble heart beats beneath a ragged vest."

I have noticed in our country towns that fewer of the boys rise to distinction than those of the country. The country boy rises early and feeds his father's stock, and hurries off to school on a winter's morning, with his cheeks as red as a rose by passing through the chilly blasts of winter. No wonder, under these circumstances, and with such a struggle to brave the storm of life, they may become great and useful men. They get the physical as well as the mental training, which is just as essential for their future happiness. Colleges have built gymnasiums for their students to take exercise, and have groves to imitate the forests; but they fall far short of these natural environments.

Also, the college boys have instituted a modern game of football, which borders just as close to heathenism as the gladiatorial shows of Greece and Rome or the arena of Mexico.

It is true that a farmer's life is not all pleasure and happiness, but it affords many useful lessons that otherwise they would not get. Country life keeps boys away from the city, until they are mature in years, and then they are not so liable to learn the many vices, and slang phrases, which the city belle and dandy delight in using for mere pastime, for want of something better for the mind to work upon. The mind should always be employed on something wholesome or useful, for it is never at rest, and if not employed it wanders on trivial things; and in the country these useful things are always at hand, varying from the most beautiful to the sublime. You will notice that the Savior, in His beautiful parables and metaphors, always used these natural illustrations, and also all writers and poets, in their sweetest songs and pithy sarcasm, drew upon the most remarkable scenes of real life as a basis for their works.

Country life instills into a person a desire for freedom, and encouraged the Boston boys to defy General Gage and the redcoats when breaking their ice; and this same spirit enthused General Andrew Jackson to decline to black an English officer's boots, for which he received a sword-cut wound that he carried to his grave. It was this same spirit and ambition which animated Horatius to hold the bridge over the Tiber, leading to Rome, against a whole army, while two men cut it in two, and he then leaped into the river and swam to shore. And it was this same love of liberty that caused the people of Rome to crown Cincinnatus king while plowing in his field with a yoke of oxen; and when he had served his mission, he resigned his kingship and returned to his home—an heroic example for the world. So if you desire a great feat to be done, or a hardship to be borne, you will be safe in leaving it to a country boy.

INTERURBAN RAILWAY.

Riding on a street car,
　Speeded by a wire—
Bless me! it is pleasant
　Riding on the flyer.

Passing on the highway,
　By the farm and dell,
Viewing many pretty things,
　Scenes I love so well.

Farmers, get you ready,
　And make this modern change;
It will enliven ev'ry product
　With which it is in range.

Transported with your produce
    To a business town,
Plenty in your pockets
    When markets quick are found.

Riding for a pittance—
    Bless me! it is fun.
Grant the needed franchise,
    And let the flyer come.

Rural transportation
    Makes a business go;
If you don't believe it,
    Try, and then you'll know.

The handy mileage station
    Accommodates the whole,
And quickens all the pulses,
    And animates the soul.

THE MODERN WOODMAN.

O Woodman! protect your wife
    From hunger and from shame;
She is the jewel of your life,
    And bears your only name.

Stand by her while you live,
    Protect her when alone;
True love to you she'll give,
    The idol of your home.

Prepare that, when you're gone,
    Plenty will be there.
The Woodman is toiling on
    With virtue pure and rare.

Let not the children cry
    And disturb a mother's breast:
Be sure that when you die,
    Your policy gives them rest.

Go join the brotherhood
    While you are hale and strong;
There's none so pure and good
    To help poor souls along.

There's plenty now in store
    For those who stand in need;
Ours is the shining shore,
    For friendship is our creed.

O neighbor! sow the seed
    Of woodcraft throughout the land;
The union is not for greed,
    But to extend a helping hand.

Let each mild zephyr blow
    Laden with rich perfume;
You by this incense know
    That friends surround your tomb.

June 8, 1904.

WHEN I WAS YOUNG.

When I was young and cheeks were fair,
I had a rustic woodland air;
I wandered o'er the shady hills,
Where bloomed the pretty daffodils—
    When I was young.

I strolled along the sparkling brook,
For shining pebbles I would look;
And many a pretty, shining shell
I found and gave to little Nell—
    When I was young.

I sought the pleasant woodbine shade,
And played " keep store " with many a maid.
This morn of life so soon was passed,
It was so sweet it could not last—
    When I was young.

In corded grapevines I would swing;
The woods with music loud did ring;
The very earth was all in tune;
'Twas just the fullness of life's noon—
    When I was young.

I went to school, a little man;
To play and romp was all my plan;
I threw sweet kisses 'cross the room
At youth and beauty, bud and bloom—
    When I was young.

But I have passed through all my teens,
Yet youthful pleasures haunt my dreams.
I'm standing by a purling brook,
In its waters I stood to look—
        When I was young.

My mind threw off its load of care,
A boy again I'm standing there;
The moon expelled the shades of night,
The shoals all gleamed with silver light—
        When I was young.

My hair is streaked with shades of gray,
No youthful pleasures now for aye.
I long for days that ne'er can come,
That once were full of joy and fun—
        When I was young.

The wings of morning passed me by,
And left me there alone to sigh
And think how oft my feet had trod
Along that brook with fishing rod—
        When I was young.

TO A BIRD.

O, sing me a song,
  Sweet bird of my choice,
And fill my dear soul
  With the notes of thy voice.

Sitting high on a bough
  As it's tilting away,
Let your sweet melody
  Be cheery to-day.

Gay and light-hearted,
  Dear friend of the wood,
Your songs so impress me
  With the lives of the good,

And bring to my memory
  The bright things of our May,
Which drive away sorrow
  As the sun lights the day.

Yet brighter and brighter
  Are our lives at our home
As the rays of pure sunshine
  In harmony are known.

Like the song of the singer,
  Our heart must be pure,
So loving, so childlike,
  If we would endure.

Inspired is the singer
Which you so much love,
And the voice of the angels
Now answers above.

OUR FATHER.

Our father sat in his easy-chair
And whiled the time away;
His hair was white as the snow to the sight,
An emblem of a better day.

His youth was like the flowers that grow
Along the purling brook:
But he's traveled sublime the sands of time,
And taken a different look.

His form was bent by the toil of years
For the ones he loved the best:
It soothed his care with blessings rare
As a treasure he saved for rest.

His children he loved, and guided each day,
And taught them lessons of good;
But they have flown to homes of their own,
Like the nestlings of the wood.

He often mused o'er things gone by,
When his wife was a bright-blooming flower.
And the children would cry for a sweet lullaby
From a voice like a falling star.

But she is gone to realms unknown,
　Where they know not of sorrow nor woe,
To rest in peace with the queens of the East,
　Where never mortal can go.

Our father—poor soul!—with tottering step,
　Still yearns for the river of life,
And is wandering at will up Zion's hill
　To meet his loved children and wife.

WHEN THE PAWPAWS ARE RIPE.

When the autumn days are coming,
　And it's getting cool o' nights,
Then I love to take a ramble,
　When the pawpaws are ripe.

When the leaves are turning golden,
　Streaked in autumn's purest dight,
Then I love to shake the bushes,
　When the pawpaws are ripe.

Then the city chaps are coming,
　With their lasses tripping light,
And they shake the clumps of bushes,
　When the pawpaws are ripe.

Then the 'possum is getting sassy,
　And his coat is not so white;
And the colored coons are hunting,
　When the pawpaws are ripe.

Then the 'possums climb the bushes,
    And they curl their tails aright
Round a limb that is richly laden,
    When the pawpaws are ripe.

Glorious scenes of loving childhood,
    When our life is pure and bright,
And we ramble in the forest
    When the pawpaws are ripe.

These are pleasures worth recalling
    To the aged ones dim of sight,
For they hear the fun and laughter
    When the pawpaws are ripe.

Like the papyrus reed of Egypt,
    These trees are passing out of sight,
And there'll be no place for hunting
    When the pawpaws are ripe.

September 16, 1900.

STICK TO YOUR CALLING.

I have wandered to the town
Where old Midas hung around
        Long ago;
And the counters, filled, o'erflowing,
Seemed like fortunes fast were growing
        By such show.

Ev'rything was neatly shining.
While the merchant was repining
   At his trade;
Newer things were always coming.
And the spindles sweet were humming
   In the shade.

But poor labor it was wanting —
Idle show is always vaunting
   In its way.
Don't believe in vain appearing.
Nor sweet stories you are hearing
   Ev'ry day.

Stick to your humble calling.
It just needs some overhauling
   For the time:
Don't believe in this or that.
Nor the fame of some grown fat
   In Klondike clime.

All will surely come out well.
As we've heard the poet tell
   To a friend;
Stick the closer to your trade.
Then your fortune will be made
   In the end.

Never let bold specters rise
To allure you otherwise
   Than the right;

They are like some wanton boys
Playing idly with their toys
  To the sight.

Rolling stones ne'er gather moss;
Like the breakers, they are tossed
  O'er the lea.
But if you would make a start,
From each day just set apart,
  Small it be.

Floating bubbles soon will burst,
And the surface look the worse
  For their life.
Little treasure can exist
By our taking too much risk
  In such strife.

The illusive Eldorado
May be swept, like a tornado,
  Far away:
But by holding to each penny,
You will have bright dollars many
  For a stay.

February 26, 1900.

MY SWEETHEART OF LONG AGO.

I once had a sweetheart—
 In my youth of long ago:
'Twas in my school days that I met her,
 And true love was wont to flow.

My heart was young and tender,
  And she was blithe and gay,
And I always sought her company
  When the time would come to play.

We would hunt the pretty mosses
  And the flowers of brilliant hue
Which were emblems of affection
  In the hearts of lovers true.
We would write our little verses,
  Which we passed across the room;
They were sweeter than the daisies
  Or the lilies full in bloom.

Ev'ry word was but a picture,
  Like a crystal in the snow—
From the heart a true inscription,
  As young lovers' hearts o'erflow.
And the kisses that I threw her
  She would answer just the same;
From her lips as pure as nectar,
  Like sweet honeydew they came.

We played many a game of ball,
  Which we called " three-cornered cat; "
And she always did the striking,
  For I would not take the bat.
She would laugh and shake her tresses
  As she shyly glanced at me,
With such pretty, roselike dimples
  On her cheeks so fair to see.

We would often "drop the kerchief."
  I ran the circuit round and round
Until I came behind my May.
  Then I dropped the kerchief down.
She had many a graceful charm,
  With brow so fair and eyes so mild:
Her life was like a rippling stream
  On which Dame Nature looked and smiled.

We would run the "circling mill,"
  And tap the chosen on the back;
Then would come a race competing,
  Running round the miller's track.
If we caught the tagging miller,
  He must still keep in the race
Until he beat the one in running
  And got within the vacant place.

"Wood tag," too, was a favorite game
  With the gayer boys and girls.
I would always watch my May,
  With her waving, glossy curls:
If she stepped upon the ground,
  She would get a gentle tap;
Then she must become the catcher
  Until she caught a heedless chap.

"Black man" then was on the schedule
  As we spent our time in play:
We would run and catch each other
  And would while the time away.

Ev'ry day was like a springtime,
  Full of many buds and flowers—
Merrymaking, full of sunshine,
  Which adorned youth's happy hours.

Often we would have a "spelling,"
  And invite our neighboring schools;
We would try our best to beat them,
  No matter what would be the rules.
We chose these times to get together
  And to meet the charming lass;
You could hear the gayest laughter
  As the bells and cutters passed.

We would hang around the doorway
  To see the boys hunt out a mate.
Some would hang on like a tether,
  And some would get a hearty shake;
Then the boys would laugh and titter
  As the girls would shy away.
Those with grit would try another,
  For their hearts were blithe and gay

Often we would have a party
  In the neighborhood around;
Ev'ry youngster in the country
  Would be there so hale and sound.
We would choose our favorite lasses
  For the tune of "weevly wheat;"
Up and down the floor we tripped it,
  Planting kisses on their cheeks.

The " miller boy " was a favorite pastime,
    With a pawn above your head;
The owner must some way redeem it
    With three yards of tape instead.
Every yard must have a marking
    With a stamp of loving bliss.
Nothing could be half so jolly
    As we gave the meting kiss.

We sometimes made a " double shovel,"
    Or a flaring " sugar bowl: "
It was a scene so fit for laughing
    As the parties took their toll;
Everything went off as lovely
    As though a rabbit's foot of charm
Played the part of merrymaking
    With the youngsters from the farm.

" Post office," too, seemed just in order,
    With two watchdogs at the door;
If the wrong one was approaching,
    Then the sentinels barked the more.
But some mail is in the office,
    And some one must go and see;
If the right one is approaching,
    The vicious curs will silent be.

But there came a day of sorrow,
    When the term of school must close,
And we little, youthful lovers
    Felt the pangs of parting woes;

And erelong there came another
　From a village by the sea,
And I never could recover
　The old love May had for me.

He was tall and very handsome,
　And his heart was full of glee;
And he stole the heart of May,
　Which I thought she had for me.
But I'll always long to see her,
　For the dart of Cupid shines
While a spark of life is glowing
　And the loving heart repines.

JENNIE'S RIDE.

Little Jennie rode a "bike"
Like an arrow down the pike.
She is blithe as any roe,
Cheeks as sweet as billet-doux.

Many a lad in passing by
Cast a look of longing eye,
And vied with envy as they passed
The charming beauty of the lass.

Now one joins the maiden's side
For a pleasant talk and ride;
They are moving on—first slow,
Then faster, faster still they go.

The speed is turning to a chase,
And many a rider joins the race:
Jennie's beauty, tried and true,
Is the idol of the crew.

JENNIE'S RIDE.

She is gaining on the crowd,
Shout on shout is heard aloud,
And the champion by her side
Is behind about a stride.

But he tries and tries in vain;
She will beat him, just the same.
Then she glanced back at her chum—
Half in earnest, half in fun.

Now they reach a country town,
Telephones had brought it down;
All are out in mass to see,
Jennie laughed so heartily.

She had beat the bandy legs,
And carried safe a crate of eggs
From her little cottage home,
Where in pleasure she did roam.

Now, you boys with head in whirl
Must never race a country girl;
For the vigor they possess
Speeds a "bike" like the express.

March 16, 1900.

"THE BARD OF ALAMO."

Illustrious living, mighty dead,
    Famous in war or peace,
Now cover your diminished head
    And let your pæons cease.
Your laurels bring, your garlands weave,
    And fitting praise bestow
Upon our modern prince of verse,
    "The Bard of Alamo."

Ye men of wisdom and renown,
　　In distant lands or near,
Who wield the scepter, wear the crown,
　　And rule by love or fear;
Give praise to him whose lines in clear
　　Exquisite cadence flow
As fresh and crisp as mountain air,
　　"The Bard of Alamo."

Ye glittering hosts of classic stars
　　That deck the sky of fame,
Welcome to your proud galaxy
　　One who deserves the name;
And e'en you lesser lights, a due
　　Appreciation show
Of him who wears the poet's crown.
　　" The Bard of Alamo."

　　　　　　　　　　　　BY A FRIEND.

THE LADIES' ATHENIAN CLUB.

All hail the ladies of Crawfordsville
　　For the noble work they do!
They seem to have the force of will
　　For the club and belles-lettres, too.
They teach the lessons as they ought,
　　As mothers fraught with care,
And bring from chaos and from naught
　　Good blessings ev'rywhere.

Athens was thought to be the place
    Of all learning and of power;
But here we find it in the chase
    And in the gilded tower.
Give your noble work renown,
    As women think they should,
And seek for knowledge in the town
    And in the sylvan wood.

Teach thy lessons by precept
    And reading precious books;
Give the mind time to reflect
    And to permeate the nooks.
Let your work go on and on,
    And bring more to the fold;
Never let a chance be gone
    But shines like a gem of gold.

Then you're building to the sky
    For women and mortal men;
Seek to win the glorious prize
    And take along your ken:
Learn to know that in our noon
    Is the time to work and build,
Before this life or setting sun
    Sinks 'neath the western hills.

January 18, 1900.

(Written for the Ladies' Athenian Club, of Crawfordsville.)

DE OL' PLANTATION.

I long fur de ol' plantation,
   Wid de mornin's cheery song,
When our massa fed and cloved us,
   And de mule jest poked along;
And we j'ined de birds in de chorus,
   As we went our labors through,
Wid de warbles ob de mornin:
   " T-la-e, t-la-e, t-la-e-hoo!"

Den we picked de downy cotton
   Wid de buxom cullud chile,
An' ol' massa kept a-trottin',
   But we's sparkin' all de while;
An' we thought about de cabin
   Whar we used to lub an' coo,
An' we played an' sung ob eb'nin's:
   " T-la-e, t-la-e, t-la-e-hoo!"

O, de blackbirds sing no sweeter
   Dan de happy cullud coon:
Dah can be no better meter
   Dan de cotton-pickin' tune.
It brings back de ol' plantation,
   Wid its scenes so clear to view;
I can hear de echoes ringin':
   " T-la-e, t-la-e, t-la-e-hoo!"

So I 'joyed myself in pleasure
   'Til ol' massa sol' my Cloe,
Den I got my traps togedder
   An' I started for Canido:
But I nebber can fergit her,
   An' de pickaninnies, too,
An' de mornin' dat I lef' her—
   " T-la-e, t-la-e, t-la-e-hoo! "

Now my heart is sad an' tender
   Fur de one I's lef' behin',
But I allers will remember
   Dat good ol' sunny clime;
But now I's sad an' lonely,
   An' my heart is throbbin', too,
For dear Cloe to jine de chorus:
   " T-la-e, t-la-e, t-la-e-hoo! "

Now I's gwine to Mississippi,
   An' hunt ol' Dixie through
For my darlin' Cloe an' Kittie,
   An' I will my lub renew,
Her lips were like molasses,
   An' my arms aroun' her flew,
An' I sung as noble Crœsus:
   " T-la-e, t-la-e, t-la-e-hoo! "

LAWTON'S BRIGADE.

Brave Lawton strove to do his best
  In peace or deadly war,
And by his men was ever blessed—
  A coward he did abhor.
The cannon boomed about his tent,
  The shrapnels whistled, too,
And through his lines they made a rent,
  But brave were the boys in blue.

The bugle call was sounded then,
  The copse was just behind;
Lawton called unto his men:
  " Fall in line! Fall in line!"
They soon obeyed the General's call
  And plied the shining steel;
A shower of American minie balls
  Made the Philippinos reel.

" Charge! Forward! Give them the bayonet!"
  Their hearts beat quick and fast.
Click, click, click!—the dagger is set,
  Then forward they go in mass.
" Steady, boys; steady, steady, steady;
  Carry your solid ranks."
They extend their lines; then all is ready;
  No chance to turn their flanks.

They meet in deadly combat there,
And fight right hand to hand;
Some are pierced through with the spear,
And some bleed on the sands.
They waver then and break away,
Our heroes follow aft';
We win again in mortal fray,
The mongrels sore we pressed.

"On, brave boys, on—on!
We mean to do or die.
A noble vict'ry you have won
Beneath this tropic sky."
A private cautioned brave Lawton then
Sharpshooters were so near;
But in the jungle or the glen,
He laughed at thought of fear.

He turned around to give commands,
Which were his last behest;
The noble soul threw up his hands,
For a ball had pierced his breast.
He fell back in a comrade's arms,
For they had loved him best
Who saw him fight, and knew his charms
Surpassed quite all the rest.

His last words were: "Push on the cause!
Think of your native land,
Which has such pure and wholesome laws,
And spurns th' oppressor's hand.

Go tell my wife that here I die
    The death of a soldier brave;
And tell her not to mourn and cry—
    We'll meet beyond the grave."

That night a woman's heart beat fast
    And throbbed at her aching breast,
As she offered up a last sad prayer
    For the one she loved the best:
" O God, wilt thou take my husband home
    To reign with the saints above,
And crown him heir around the throne,
    Where Christ is light and love?"

That mother now is left alone,
    An ideal nation's love:
A light has all around her shone,
    Which does our blessings prove.
She ne'er can want, for gen'rous hands
    Are ready to bestow
All the gifts of a Christian land
    On one who met the foe.

January 30, 1900.

THE POET.

The poet lives in thoughts above
    The blue ethereal sky;
His thoughts are close akin to love
    When Nature meets his eye.

He fancies many a thing of art
 Beyond the sculptor's hand;
Grand and noble, pure at heart,
 The greatest gift to man.

Things which please are at his will,
 And colored highly, too:
He must portray them mirrored still
 To the patient reader's view.

He goes beyond the av'rage soul,
 Where saints immortal reign,
And hears sweet songs of music roll,
 And joins the sweet refrain.

He peers in space just as it were
 A fairy's golden lane,
Traveled by some sea nymphs rare,
 And gives to each a name.

Inspired are they who sing sweet lays
 By the great invisible choir,
Who write and sing in holy praise
 To the echoes of David's* lyre.

Born they are with songs of cheer
 In words of sweetest rhythm,
Breathing melodies to the ear
 So near akin to heaven.

February 8, 1900.

---

* David is the oldest poet known.

A SONNET.

The mill of time grinds slowly,
Yet it grinds both great and small.
From the pressure of the fall,
Where the rushing waters flow,
Onward, onward, it will go
To the deep, unfathomed sea.
Grinding, grinding it will be
Where the pearl and rubies glow;
Yet there must come time to rest.
When the Master grinds the grist
And the flour is made just so.
In the good we find the best—
Not a mixed or speckled list,
Like the mill that grinds below.

January 30, 1900.

OUR BABY.

Little baby in the crib,
Playing nicely with his bib.
He is pretty, I declare,
With such flowing curly hair;
Just the image of his ma.
Blue eyes shining like his pa;
He will coo a little song.
Happy elfin all day long.

O, the pretty dimpled cheeks!
Mamma kiss 'em 'cause they're sweet.
Lips like ruby—glowing, too—
Just as sweet as honeydew:
Light is beaming from his eyes,
Shine like sparkles in the sky—
A little cherub from above,
Purest tie of family love.

Look up, baby, let me see
Our sweet darling full of glee,
Playing in his willow cot,
Sweetest little forget-me-not.
Like a rose we cherish him,
Tap him lightly on the chin.
Then he will look up and coo—
Brighter days we never knew.

Play on, baby: let us see;
You're as pure as angels be.
Jabbering as he tries to talk,
Feet a-longing for to walk.
Stand up, darling: do not fear;
Take a step for mamma, dear.
But he topples and will fall:
First the baby learns to crawl.

Guy or Clarence is his name:
Angels brought him as they came
From the dotted starry sky
For his mamma's longing eye.

He will fondle on her breast,
With her arm about him pressed.
Never can a sunbeam fall,
But it shines a light for all.

February 12, 1900.

LIFE.

Life is like a bubbling spring
    Flowing onward as a brook,
With myriad voices echoing
    Along its course from ev'ry nook ;
Yet smoothly flow the waters by
    Where grasses grow and gently wave,
The wind blows calmly with a sigh
    Where fishes bask and children lave.

Beautiful scenes lie along the stream
    As you travel down the living fount,
A shining light in the distance gleams
    As the purling waters are tossed about.
Now 'tis running eddy-smooth,
    Anon 'tis dashing onward down,
And, chafing in its narrow groove,
    A voice is heard of murm'ring sound.

So it is with the living soul
    Moving onward o'er the brake,
Striving, yearning to reach the goal,
    Like the river to the lake.

It must pass some stony place,
  Where breakers heave and billows toss;
So near akin to the human race,
  No life endures without some loss.

Dewdrops sparkle in the sun,
  A gleam of light shines in the deep,
No time to rest till life is run
  And it has gone where sages sleep.
So the river runs its way
  Onward, onward to the sea;
Never can it stop and say:
  " I'm content, so let me be."

Let us do our might to-day,
  Time well spent is never lost;
Light of heart and always gay
  Will save the ship where breakers toss.
Stand at the helm and watch the fate
  Of those who never look for flaws,
And keep in view the Beautiful Gate,
  Observing pure Nature's laws.

So runs the stream of life alway
  To reach the mystic realm above,
Still achieving, still we may,
  Where hearts are full of perfect love.
Never let vague phantoms rise
  To mar the ties of friendship true;
But wing thy way beyond the skies,
  Where Christ i* glory beckons you.

February 24, 1900.

POETS ARE BORN, NOT MADE.

Worry we may, if we wish,
   At the favoritism displayed;
No use to kick 'gainst the pricks,
   For poets are born, not made.

The Muses, so lavish with favors,
   With garlands and crowns have arrayed
The children of favored Montgomery,
   For poets are born, not made.

The place of our birth condemns us,
   The gods would lend us no aid:
Parnassus slopes up from Montgomery,
   And poets are born, not made.

We reverence do to " Old Wabash,"
   We would walk in her classical shade:
But she is unable to help us,
   For poets are born, not made.

We've tried it again and again,
   For inspiration we've prayed;
But failure our portion forever,
   For poets are born, not made.

O, happy, happy Montgomery!
   Till our debt to Nature be paid
We never shall cease to regret
   That poets are born, not made.

Write it in letters of fire,
In letters that never can fade—
Yes, letters of fire will answer—
That poets are born, not made.

THE BUGGY.

If you desire a buggy
To ride and give you rest,
You should buy an "A" grade;
It certainly is the best.

It is just a dandy,
If you desire to call
And escort your best girl
To a country ball.

You have nothing for to fear,
It is so good and strong:
It is on a perfect gear,
You swiftly glide along.

The wheels are shining, glist'ning,
Humming as they run:
The boys are all a-hustling,
Want to buy them one.

Then they are contented,
Happy, it does seem:
Plenty of caresses
Just behind the screen.

"BEN HUR" IN DRAMA.

James B. Elmore, the poet of the brakes and braes of bonnie Ripley, was in town the other day, and left a few verses at the Journal office. "I offer these as a tribute to Lew. Wallace," said he, "as I want to encourage cordiality and fellowship among the literati of this part of the country. There is no reason why we should not live together as brothers and kindred spirits, as our tastes and aspirations and work are along the same lines. I do not know the General very well yet; but as soon as I get my corn under cover and poison a few pesky ground hogs that are raising hob out on the farm, I am coming in and establish the *entente cordiale.* I want to give the General all the encouragement I can, and I wrote these pleasant lines out to boost 'Ben Hur' on the stage and to let folks know that there is no meanness or jealousy among literary men such as is found among other professions." The poem goes like this:

" Halloo, Benjamin Hur! Where goest thou?"
" Like a divorced wife, to the stage just now."
" What is to be done, that you are so arrayed?"
" The show has just begun in dress parade.

You know that in the arena I fame have won,
So on the stage the race I'll run;
Bring on the orchestra and start the play,
And behold my steeds so fleet and gay."

Grasp those lines, old hero, sir,
And show us the mettle of Benjamin Hur.
Melchisedec of old had no more praise,
With no beginning of time nor end of days.

THE RACE OF BEN HUR.

Behold the chariot wreathed in gold,
And the clashing of armor as of old;
The gayest steeds are hitched to the pole,
And quick to the contest the race to unfold.

Now in the arena Benjamin great laurels has won,
The wreath of honor to him was flung;
And many were they who tried to compete
With the chieftain in this most wonderful feat.

Hurrah, hurrah! They go, and Benjamin is forcing
   ahead;
Cheer after cheer was echoed with fear as faster and
   faster they sped—
The most beautiful scene that one could behold,
And the race of Ben Hur will ever be told.

The horses are running with nostrils spread wide—
O say, isn't it a beautiful glide?
There goes the hero, with streamers of red,
The length of his chariot in distance ahead.

Waneda, his darling, is waving a sign
As the hero is passing the three-quarter line;
But Messala—poor fellow!— is lying aground,
For Bennie has hubbed him and turned him
   around.

He is speeding ahead and cannot look back,
Wild echoes are ringing in the wake of his track,
And yet he is nudging the steeds all the time
Until he has reached the end of the line.

No rag-time race will he ever run,
For now is the time his laurels are won;
And many bouquets are tossed to the sage,
And, kneeling, he is crowned as king of the stage.

The race is completed with echoing cheer;
The horses were running, the people did fear;
And the hero is standing in his chariot aright
And pulling the reins like the string of a kite.

" Whoa, brave boys: whoa, I say!
Where is our rival, I pray? "
He is lying back there in a pool of his gore,
Never again to race any more.

Hurrah for Ben Hur!   Hurrah for the race!
Hurrah for Lew. Wallace, who started the chase
And gave us this play—the best of the age—
The grandest of scene that is now on the stage!

A SONNET.

The rose that shines with brightest hue
And nods with splendor in the breeze
Is the most beautiful thing to please;
But 'tis known it only drew
Its richness from the place it grew,
Down in the little sunny dell,
Where little brooklets leap and swell
While passing onward gently through.
So it is with mortal man,
Passing onward o'er the shoal,
Freighted with best riches known,
Gathering stores where'er he can,
Things which make a perfect soul,
Building of a perfect home.

ACROSTIC.

Many a precious little thought
Adores the one for which I sought.
Rambling is my mind at rest ;
Youthful pleasures are the best.

All along the sands of time,
No one knows the heart sublime ;
No one knows the aches of mine,

Everlasting to endure.
Leisurely I sought the pure.
Memory now recalls anew
Orange blossoms tried and true ;
Roses bloom and brighter grow,
Engraved on my memory so.

WHAT THE HOOSIER SEES IN CHICAGO.

The Hoosier goes to Chicago
  To see the sights, and then
He treasures up his heart's delights
  And then comes home again.
The first that meets the longing eyes
  Is the smoke from a thousand flues,
And next you see the rolling tide
  Of the lake and waving sloughs ;

Statues of our bravest men
  And monuments of pride.
Their sarcophagus laid beneath
  The image steed they ride ;

A legion of all-colored lights
    In names and divers shapes—
'Tis like the starry galaxy
    When ev'rything's in state.

There are bridges of quaint design,
    And aqueducts so grand,
And arches at the ending streets,
    Where people throng the strand
And watch the vessels coming in
    Of all the different kinds:
The little bark which plies the lake
    Recalls our boyhood times.

The lighthouse standing in the deep
    And twinkling like a star
Is to the inland observer new,
    His mind goes out afar.
The buildings, too, above your head
    Will make you gasp and sigh—
When you are in the Masonic Temple,
    Just twenty-two stories high.

The Great Northern Hotel is grand indeed,
    Its organ pipes aloud;
'Tis like the rolling thunder's echo
    Along the distant cloud.
Then there is a beautiful place
    With palms and music to please:
Its name is just " Blue Ribbon Saloon,"
    Its frequenters it will deceive.

The Board of Trade is an exciting place,
    You cannot hear at all;
Their voices change from high to low
    As the margins rise and fall.
Some go broke, and some have made,
    And some still bid away;
And some possess a wan, sad face,
    Expressed by "Alackaday!"

You pass along to Lincoln Park,
    The grandest place of yore;
A perfect earthly paradise,
    With treasures rich in store.
There are water ways and acqueducts,
    And plants from every zone
Inside a grand glass crystal palace,
    And thrive just like at home.

The museum, too, is fraught with things
    And many curious arts—
A perfect school to observing men,
    Developing their minds and hearts.
Along the boulevard the hansoms run
    And carry the " upper crust,"
While the common people walk along
    And view Tecumseh's bust.

There stands the novel Ferris Wheel,
    A band of human freight:
'Tis propelled by sprocket wheels
    At a thirty-minute rate.

You see all this on any day,
  And many other scores;
The toper, too, has hilarious times
  When vice has open doors.

You meet the people on the street;
  They talk in divers ways—
Some with accent on the " r's,"
  And some are on the " a's."
It seems to be a Babel new
  The heavens soon to reach,
Where God Almighty did diffuse
  The different kinds of speech.

ACROSTIC.

Just a little pleasure
Essential to our care;
Rays of brightest sunshine,
Rays so rich and rare.
You possess a brilliant life;
Knowing it is true,
Evenly you scan the right,
Especially the new;
Nothing can obstruct the sight
Your optic pierces through.

ACROSTIC.

All is not gold that glitters,
Long with brilliancy it may shine:
Beautiful things are mixed with bitter.
Even in garb of dress sublime.
Rich it is to glow with brightness.
Touch of Nature pure and kind:

Cunning art but still and sightless.
Unobserved in chambered mind.
Now and then the light reflected
Nearer brings the thinking soul—
In our minds far retrospected
Nigh unto the starting goal.
Gayer then, no thoughts but leisure:
Heavy loads were slight and rare:
All our thoughts were fraught with pleasure.
Manhood attained, some burdens share.

SUGAR-MAKING SONG.

When the frost begins to slacken
    And old Winter has lost his grip,
Then the maples quit their cracking
    And the sap begins to drip.
You can hear the pitter-patter
    In the vessel down below,
As the little droplets clatter
    In a circling tidal flow.

'Tis a sweet and flowing nectar,
    Like the wine that Jupiter sips,
And I love to be inspector
    As I press it to my lips :
And we fill the tankards flowing
    Till it sparkles as of old,
And the bubbles keep a-glowing
    With a tint of shining gold.

The south wind joins the chorus
    In the songs of humming bees,
And the blue jay flits before us
    In the swinging boughs of trees.
And the violets nod at leisure
    As they bloom down by the brink,
And the chipmunk skips at pleasure
    In the secret hidden chink.

And as cooler grows the evening,
    There will icicles grow
As the sap is slowly leaving
    The spiles in gentle flow ;
And the downy-budded willows
    That are standing by the brook
Are reflected in the shallows
    With a sort of silver look.

Then the screech owl shrieks a whistle
    In a solemn sort of way,
And the goldfinch on the thistle
    Sings a song of parting day :

Then the camp fire shines the brighter
  As the sparks in myriads rise,
And all hearts are gay with laughter
  As the darkness dims our eyes.

Then the hick'ry torches sputter
  As we change them in our hands;
'Long the road the fire we scatter
  From the glowing, shining brands.
Then the mud will splash and spatter,
  But it matters not, you see;
It just takes this clash and clatter
  For the youthful cup of glee.

Men are wont to sing in praises
  Of their youth of long ago,
When their hearts were full of graces
  And the sweetest blessings flow;
But the toil of passing years
  Shows upon their furrowed brow,
And with sadness blends a tear
  As they think of then and now.

SUGAR MAKING.

Haul out the kettles and place the metal
  O'er a fiery furnace 'neath;
Your hands will nettle as the mortar you settle
  And make their casing sheath.

Bring on some stone and build a cone
    To carry the smoke above;
Then you have known a sugar home,
    Which children dearly love.

SUGAR MAKING.

Go tap the trees—'twill give you ease—
    And place the vessels below;
There are rhythm-tu-rees and honeybees
    When the sap begins to flow.

Rat-tat-tat!—you hear the pat
   Of the nectar striking below:
There is a pit-a-pat and a sound like that
   As we gather it to and fro.

The children scout and run about,
   And sip the flowing sweets:
They pick the route and gayly shout
   When in such pleasant retreats.
There are turkey pease and childish glees,
   And moss from brake and braes;
We cry aloud and join the crowd
   And sing in childish ways.

The goldfinch's flight is our delight
   Across the heath and wood;
We turn and look in every nook,
   As children think they should.
The squirrel, too, from his burrow flew,
   And slyly kind o' hid;
We climbed the tree and tried to see
   What little Bunny did.

Our fathers toil and kettles boil.
   Sweet-scented is the steam;
We children foil a chance so royal
   And watch the kettles teem.
We stir the wax until it cracks,
   Then pour it out to cool:
Its strands relax like breaking flax,
   When pulling, as a rule.

When the sirup puffs, it is enough,
　　The sugar-making degree;
You stir the stuff with ladle rough,
　　Then granulated 'twill be.
The sugar is made and work is stayed,
　　The refining is surely done.
We think it paid for what we made
　　Sweet dreams of childish fun.

These youthful days we always praise
　　As being the gem of life;
The water ways and roundelays
　　Never knew of toil and strife.
The violets blue and maidens true
　　All sung with gentle strain;
Their hearts all knew sweet anthems, too;
　　Their echoes still remain.

The warp and woof was our behoof,
　　The sun the shuttle plied,
The vaulted roof was high aloof
　　Where the solar planets glide.
The new of the moon is the harvest tune
　　When the sap runs best, they say;
But the wily coon won't tap too soon,
　　For the wood just dries away.

January 10, 1900.

11

ACROSTIC.

Just a little witty
Erases much of gloom;
Sure, it makes a ditty
Sweet road to royal bloom.
Ease is not a pleasure.

Greatness makes a man;
Rare as is our leisure,
Energy shows a hand;
Esteem is a golden measure
Now known in ev'ry land.

ABIGE AND TURKEY TOM.

Come, old Tom, let's have some fun,
    And play around about;
I will go, then you may come
    And join me on the route.

You shake your head and gobble, too,
    As big as any man;
I'll catch you by the neck, if you
    Will only bravely stand.

Ker-ert! ker-ert!—you're talking, too;
    1 do not understand.
You bugaboo, I'll throw at you;
    You've pecked me on the hand.

Now sidle off and come again,
  With dangling red goatee;
You think you'll boss now, if you can,
  Or cockerel fight with me.

ABIGE AND TURKEY TOM.

Come on, old boy; I'm ready now,
  And give the starting shout.
He sallied in—I don't know how—
  And got me on the snout.

Now, you see, it isn't fair
  To strike below the waist,
Or pull my flowing curly hair,
  Or pick me in the face.

Then I thought I'd start and run
  As fast as I could sail;
The gobbler, too, joined in the fun
  And caught my jacket tail.

Then mamma came, with broom in hand,
  To stop the running fight.
And wielded it as women can,
  And loudly laughed outright.

He stood aloof and gobbled loud,
  As though he'd won the fight;
He strutted round like Lucifer proud—
  A showy, gaudy sight.

January 16, 1900.

MUSIC.

Music is the science and art of musical tones or of
musical sounds. From the earliest stages of an-
tiquity there seems to have been some kind of music
to blend with the sympathies of appreciative man.
You may go among any of the peoples of the world,
and they will have some kind of music. The orients,
or ancients, used principally the musical harp, such
as David played in the presence of the remorseful
king for his amusement. We read in the sacred
writings of vocal and instrumental music. We have
different kinds of music to affect or influence the different feelings of mankind. The cheerful or lively
music animates the soul of the young and brings
every nerve and muscle into motion and satisfies their
childlike nature. Then we have the solemn or sacred music, which so affects the soul or inward man
to its more tender sympathies. Even the savages
have some kind of music to meet their necessities;
they must have it in their councils of war and of
peace. And civilized man, in time of a nation's
greatest peril, may hesitate to take up his country's
cause; but when the fife plays and the drum beats the
call to enlist, he can resist no longer, but is ready to
face death, if need be, by the inspiration these instru-
ments have imparted to him.

There is no living thing which has a voice but
makes some tone of the musical scale. It is a pleas-

ure to listen to the beautiful birds as they hold their morning matinées, giving us a very pleasing variety of their sweet, musical voices. Even the cawing crow plays an important part in the harmonious world, but it remains for the mocking bird to fill one's soul with rapture and delight.

Music has almost magical effect upon some animals as well as man. You can notice that they either show signs of delight or remorse. The faithful dog may set up a pitiful howl on hearing music, which in some way affects his nervous system, and even reptiles will show an uneasiness on hearing certain strains of music.

It remains for civilized man to perfect the scale of music. The modern organ and pianoforte reach the top of the scale when the beautiful pieces of modern music are rendered, so rich and sublime, so delightful to the human soul.

Next to pure life, music is calculated to make man happy. The hearing of good music shapes our hearts to love God and man better; and if clouds of gloom or despondency come over us, music will bring back the beautiful rays of sunlight and make us again happy and glad that we live in such a harmonious world as this, with such beautiful strains of music blending in harmony and making the heart of man so light and cheery. It is so like love, the golden cord which binds the heart of man to the throne of God.

The world has had some great authors who wrote
and played under very trying circumstances. Beethoven, whose windows of the soul were closed to the
beauties of Nature, led a very useful life. He wrote
many excellent pieces of music which will live forever.
In old age, having been driven from home, he was
traveling through Germany, and, unknown, stopped
at a house and begged lodging. In the evening a
young lady played and sung one of his most wonderful productions, and he exclaimed: " I wrote that
music!" He made himself known to them, and died
at that home, nursed by their tender hands and honored as one of the world's greatest pilgrims and musicians. Robert Schumann was educated for a lawyer.
Disliking that profession, he learned to play music;
but one of his fingers being defective, he learned to
write music, and he so fascinated a young lady musi-
sian upon whom he called to play his productions
that she married him, and so combined two of the
world's most renowned people. But, like Beethoven,
he was very unfortunate, for the great productions
which he wrote so wrought upon him that he lost his
mind; but his loving partner never deserted him,
and well proved woman's fidelity and devotion to one
of the greatest of modern musicians.

The female voice is the most perfect of all vocal
music, and is so wonderful and pleasing to the soul.

Andre, the explorer, had his wife sing in a phono-
graph, so that he could hear her sweet, musical voice

when he was taking his fatal trip to the Arctic regions. We have often read of the sweet sirens who
sung so beautifully as to lure the unwary sailors to
the dangers of the lonely isles, from whence they
never returned.

National airs played in time of war make men
face deadly foes when otherwise they might fear
their task. After the battle at El Caney, Cuba, the
wounded were taken to the battle ships, and the bands
began to play "The Star-spangled Banner," and
many a dying soldier shouted and waved his hands
for the Union flag and his country as he drew his
last faint breath. Men, when their hearts are filled
with good music, are inspired to do greater and nobler
deeds. The poor blind beggar in the street depends
upon how he moves the hearts of his fellows by his
touching songs for contributions and aid.

HOW SUCCESS IS WON.

Solomon, the wisest of all earthly kings, has said: "Train up a child in the way he should go: and when he is old, he will not depart from it." That was true in his day, and is also true in ours. Nature has endowed us with bodies, minds, wills, and judgment capable of any undertaking. The philosopher who was captured by unlearned men said, "Give me time and I will extricate myself." He was depending on the power which the God of Nature had given him. So it must be with us, if we fulfill our mission in this world. A person must lay his plans, and then work according to them with a determined will. Some people, because they achieve great things, are proclaimed geniuses and looked upon as wonderful men: but it is only because they have made use of the powers which were in them. All men are created equal or nearly so, but some tower above their fellows, like the giant oak of the forest, on account of their great energy and perseverance. The lines of Longfellow well illustrate the fact:

"The heights by great men reached and kept
  Were not attained by sudden flight:
But they, while their companions slept,
  Were toiling upward in the night."

By "success" we mean not only those who have heaps of gold and silver, bonds and stocks, but also those who have accomplished the things which they set out to attain. Some desire to become great scholars and teachers and to be benefactors to the people and nation; and if they attain to their aim, then they are a wonderful success, to be remembered forever. Some may desire to study for the ministry and spend their days for the cause of Christianity, like Luther, Calvin, and Huss, spending their time not all in pleasure, but sometimes being obliged to sing in the streets for bread to allay their hunger, and also being hunted by the crowned heads of Europe, that they might persecute them. But listen to the words of Luther when summoned to Worms for trial because his teaching was different from that of the clergy. His friends warned him not to go, but he exclaimed: " I would go, if there were as many devils in Worms as the tiles on the roof! " And he did go.

" Thrice is he armed who hath his quarrel just."

These men were a success, for they accomplished what they set out to do, and more, for their works still live. Their books are but phonographs of the dead, speaking to us of their trials, loves, joys, and deeds, which are as wholesome as the air that blows.

We have examples of self-made men, and by all odds all are self-made or never made. Even the student at college must study or fail. Many go through college and pass out of sight. They are a disappointment to themselves and their friends; they have not the will, push, nor energy to carry themselves on to victory. But look at Abraham Lincoln, how differently he obtained his education—at the fireside by the light of a candle after he had labored hard all day long. He saw beauty in Nature; his feelings were in sympathy with what he did, or he never could have accomplished what he did. He had tender feelings for others, and so became the emancipator of the slaves of our republic. His name still lives and will live to the end of time. He is an example—one of the most wonderful—of the self-made men of the world, but there are thousands of others. A few years ago the State of New York sent out West a car load of orphan boys to find homes wherever they could and to seek a living, and it so happened that two boys sat in the same seat—one a large, fine-featured fellow, and the other a small, undersized lad—and when they arrived at their destination, the farmers came in to pick out boys whom they thought most suitable for work. It so happened that the little fellow was left until the last, on account of his size; it seemed as though no one wanted him; but a sturdy Irishman came along and took pity on him and gave him an apple, telling him that, if no one wanted him, he might go home with him; and so he did; and to-day those two boys who sat in the same seat and were like the stone which the builders rejected are governors in two of our Western States. All of this was achieved by courage, pluck, and energy. The fortune of a father or mother is no royal road to suc-

cess, for it may be wafted away at a single stroke of
the pen; but courage like Leonidas had at the pass
of Thermopylæ, with his little army, may move the
world. Energy is the only true road to success, but
energy out of use is dead. Napoleon Bonaparte gave
the nations of Europe a great deal of trouble on account of his indomitable will and courage.

Nations, too, are like individuals according to their
energy and push. It is easy to see the status of the
United States, if we but look at the Spanish-Ameri-
can War and our valiant soldiers knocking at the
walls of China, which were like a parapet of earth to
them.

Some desire great wealth as a road to fame. It is
not always the best kind of riches one can possess,
but it is very necessary in civilized nations to have
money to carry on the business of the nation; and
the more of it they have, the more prosperous it will
be. Money promotes trade and civilization; heathen
lands have no use for it. Some trades and occupa-
tions could not be carried on without it. Still, we
have individuals who make a wrong use of it; but it
cannot be said that they were not a financial success.
They cannot be rated with such men as Johns Hopkins, who endowed Johns Hopkins University, and
Simon Yandez, who gave $50,000 to build a library
at Crawfordsville, Ind.

We have had great men like S. F. B. Morse, who in-
vented telegraphy; but he lacked the means to carry

it into effect, and had to ask the government to aid him, thereby receiving $30,000 to bring his invention before the people. Elias Howe was another who strove to gain achievement in poverty and distress; but success came at last, as it will to the obedient, diligent, and persevering. Goodyear, Fulton, and Whitney were the laughingstock for the common herd, being branded as fools by them; but success crowned their efforts, and then they were the pride of the world, while the scoffers have passed from earth unknown; no lasting monument marks their departure in the minds of men. If one desires to succeed in a pecuniary sense, he will have to stop all unnecessary spending of money, and he can soon own a good home of his own; for just think when you spend a nickel for a cigar, it would buy a square yard of land worth fifty dollars per acre, and the purchase of a bottle of pop would buy another, and a glass of wine or ale would buy two square yards, and so by avoiding such expenditures for a few years you can be in good circumstances.

Jay Gould was once a poor boy, and he spent his first fifty cents for a book to carry to school, and then we find him sitting in the street hungry for something to eat; but these were trials which taught him the value of money. Then we soon find him in a tannery, a bank, and then in one of the greatest stock exchanges of the world, having ascended from the bottom of the ladder to the top by his own effort.

One must always be on the alert and watchful to take
in the situation when it offers, or all is lost. A good
epitaph for some who are always disappointed in their
efforts would be: ".A little too slow." Men are a
little like race horses, and the most observant, dili-
gent, and frugal wins the race.

> Let us live as noble men,
> 　Working for a crown above;
> Let us live as best we can,
> 　Full of virtue, peace, and love.
>
> Strive to gain a rich reward,
> 　And let the vain world know
> We are children of the Lord,
> 　Born in worlds below.
>
> Be up and doing with a will,
> 　With a heart both pure and great;
> Climb the roughest rugged hill,
> 　Then success will be your fate.
>
> Never stop as laggards do,
> 　Looking sad, disconsolate;
> To yourself be bold and true,
> 　You will be among the great.
>
> Monuments will speak your fame
> 　On the bold, emblazoned page;
> Children long will lisp your name
> 　In a future coming age.

Never falter at the top,
  Let your course go on and on ;
Running rivers ne'er can stop,
  Lest their force is lost and gone.

Nature's purest waters glide
  O'er their shining pebbly shore ;
Blooming flowers line each side,
  Lending sweetness as of yore.

Write your name so all may know,
  Passing onward as they may,
That true worth is not a show,
  But a crown that shines by day.

ENVOY.

May we always love sweet poetry, friend,
  As it pleases you and me ;
May we meet some other time again
  This side of eternity.